To:
Mrs. Jones

Make reading & learning!
a lifelong journey!

THE TIME STANDS STILL
CHRONICLES

Mystery in Time

Hope you like
the story!

By D.A. Lee

D.A. Lee

11-24-15

The Time Stands Still Chronicles: Mystery in Time
By D.A. Lee

Published by Time Stands Still Press, LLC
www.TimeStandsStillChronicles.com

Time Stands Still Press books are available from Ingram Press and can be ordered through the Ingram Press catalog.

Cover Design and Layout by Launchpad Press, Cody, WY
www.launchpad-press.com

LCCN: 2012943707

ISBN-13: 978-0-9846-9570-6

DEDICATION

To Dad, who showed me by example to like everyone.

ACKNOWLEDGMENTS

A special thanks to my incredible wife, Susan, who allowed me time away as well as time at home to write.

Thanks to Tom Bird who showed me how to find the Author Within.

PROLOGUE

GRAMMA TESSIE HAD ARRIVED AT GRAMS' AT ALMOST THE same time as Dr. Emory, who was getting out of his car when she pulled into the circle driveway. They walked in together. Grams was waiting for them seated in the front living room of the old farmhouse.

They greeted Grams cordially and Dr. M asked if the place had been swept for listening devices. Gramma Jamison (Grams) said she had been checking every hour since he had called. "I also have turned on the jamming system we brought from Saros."

Gramma Tessie spoke next. "I drove twenty miles roundabout through Hayward on my way here. Then I came in on the old gravel road, all five miles of it! I turned on the signal transceiver and watched the skies. My special high-altitude blocker was also activated. So no one followed me and no one saw me come here."

"So then we are ready to begin," Dr. M stated more as a command than in a matter-of-fact sort of voice.

As he sat down, slowly his features changed. His ears grew slightly larger and his head became a bit more elongated up and down. His skin turned a bronze color and a slight glow seemed to emanate from his entire body. The grandmothers experienced the same changes. These three had much to discuss and plan for at this meeting. The future of Saros and maybe even Earth depended on decisions they were about to make.

1

I T ALL STARTED ABOUT FOUR WEEKS AGO. MIKE AND J.J., BOTH sixth graders and best friends, were exploring in the basement at J.J.'s grandmother's old farmhouse, a few miles into the country. J.J.—Johnny Jacob Jamison —is just about your average sixth grader. He has dark hair, thick and bushy. His build is solid but not heavy set. A sort of round face accented by dimples in each cheek makes him attractive to the girls, although he has no interest in them. His easy manner and quiet confidence help him make friends easily, and he is also a very good student.

J.J. lives with his mother and younger brother, Jerry. Their family was at the center of a big mystery just over two years ago. Harold Jamison, the head of their family, disappeared without a trace. The police investigated thoroughly. No one had seen anything. He seemed to have vanished from the face of the earth.

J.J., Jerry, and their mom have been continuing to adjust to their loss and have moved on with their lives.

They continue to wonder what happened. They are sure that someday the mystery will be solved. At least that is their hope.

Mike Hollywell is J.J.'s cousin and best friend. Mike is a little taller than most sixth graders. Being somewhat slim doesn't detract from the fact that he is very strong. He has great endurance. Athletics is something he excels at while maintaining straight As in all his classes. He can outrun anyone at his school in either short or long distances. Playing soccer and basketball are two of his favorite activities. A skilled chess player, Mike is looking forward to middle school and being a part of the chess team.

"I don't like it down here!" shouted Mike. "Why is it so dark? Aren't there any lights down here? I want to go back up."

"Oh, come on," replied J.J., shining his flashlight on Mike. "Why are you being such a crybaby? There's nothing to be afraid of. My mom and Grams are right upstairs."

"Does that light work?" Mike asked, pointing to an overhead bulb.

"I'll pull the string and see." Sure enough a little light shone from it casting strange shadows all over the room. "Is that better?"

"Not much. I still don't know why we're down here. Are we looking for something?"

"Nope. We're just exploring. I'm going through

that open doorway into the next room. I brought along a flashlight. I'll shine it in there to see if there is another light we can turn on. I think Grams said she used to keep her canned goods in there. It was dark and much cooler than the upstairs pantry behind the kitchen. Now that she can't climb stairs anymore, I'll bet no one has been down here in years."

"Why don't we keep it that way?" said Mike, and he stopped dead in his tracks. "I'm staying right here by this light and the stairs." It was three o'clock in the afternoon and even though the stairway was open and there was a wall of windows facing the outside next to the stairs, the sun was getting low in the sky on the other side of the old farmhouse. It was quite dark in there.

"Hey, scaredy-cat. How about I give you a flashlight, too?"

"Why didn't you give me one to start with?"

"I wanted to see how brave you were. You're such a big, strong boy!" J.J. added mockingly.

"Come over here and I'll give you the flashlight." As soon as Mike entered the room, J.J. turned off his flashlight and screamed.

"*Yeowee!* Don't move!"

"I'm too scared to move." Suddenly the flashlight came back on, and J.J. let out a great big belly laugh.

"Did you do that on purpose?"

"Yup. I sure got you! But I won't tell anyone about it."

J.J.'s mom came out and looked down the stairs. "Are you guys all right? I thought I heard a scream."

"No problem, Mom. I was just trying to scare Mike, that's all."

"No more screams. You'll upset Grams."

"Okay, Mom. Thanks for checking on us."

"Yeah, thanks a lot, J.J.," commented Mike. "You must think you're really funny."

"Come off it, Mike. You would have done the same thing to me if you'd had the chance."

"You got that right. Are we done now? Can we go back upstairs?"

"No. There's another small room behind this one. I want to see what's in it. You can stay here if you like."

"No way. I'm going with you. Can I have a flash-light now?"

"Sure, here it is. Now you can be really brave."

As they went through the next doorway into a small, long room, they saw many old suitcases stacked hap-hazardly against the wall. The room was only about fifteen feet long and around six feet wide. There was no window in this room, and it was very dark.

"I want to get a closer look at these old suitcases." As J.J.'s eyes moved down the stack following his flash-light beam, he noticed what looked like an old trunk with straps around it. "I want to pull that old trunk out. Shine your light over here."

"Okay, but I'm not touching anything. Do you

think there might be snakes or something down here?"

"I doubt it. I don't see any mouse tracks or rat dung. The basement is sealed pretty tight, so there appears to be no snake food down here."

J.J. slowly and carefully lifted the boxes and suitcases and moved them aside. He was surprised when he saw what good shape the trunk was in. "I'm going to open this and see what's inside. It has my great-grandfather's initials on it, RJJ. That stands for Rolland Jacob Jamison. He built this farmhouse and raised livestock here for many years. My mom and Grams told me about what a hard worker he was. He was also a very respected man in the community."

He pulled the trunk out a little ways and both boys lit it up with their flashlights. "Go ahead and open it," Mike dared.

J.J. carefully undid the old leather straps. They were surprisingly strong and in good shape. Slowly he opened the lid. The only things inside appeared to be some old textbooks. They were packed in pretty tight. He had to wedge his fingers under one of the books to get it to come out.

One of the books had the same initials as the ones on the outside of the trunk.

"Look at this, Mike. Here are my great-grandpa's initials on a book." As he opened the book, he noticed that it was a Bible. "This must have been Great-grandpa Jamison's personal Bible. Wow!" J.J. exclaimed.

"Here are similar initials on a large-sized family Bible. These are probably Great-grandma Jamison's initials. I wonder if Grams knows these books are down here. They're still in nice shape."

"Are you ready to go back upstairs now?" Mike asked.

"Wait a minute. I found a brown envelope stuck between the Old and New Testaments. It's got 'To my first great-grandson' written on it. Do you think this was left for me? I'm the only first great-grandson I know of."

"Could be. Let's take it upstairs and open it and see what it says. Maybe it contains money or a treasure map!"

"Nah, I doubt that. I think I'll just stick it in my pocket and wait until I get home to look at it. Keep holding the light while I put these books back into the trunk. I'll leave the Bible on top so we can easily get to it if we need to. I'd like to tell Grams about it after I see what's in the letter."

When they had finished securing the trunk, J.J. piled a couple of boxes on top of it. Then they made their way back through the basement, up the stairway, and through the door into the house. Grams and Mom were sitting in the front living room talking.

"Did you guys find anything interesting?" Grams asked, smiling. "You sure made a lot of noise down there." Grams may be old but she still had very good hearing.

"Nothing to speak of," replied J.J. "We were just looking around. It sure is dusty and dirty down there. Does anyone ever go down there?"

"No," Grams replied. "I used to when I still canned a lot, but it's been years since I've been down there."

"We'll do some more searching around next time we're here. Where's Jerry?"

"He's on the front porch reading his new book. I think he lives the stories as he reads them. He has such a wonderful imagination," Mom said, and smiled.

"Grams, is it okay if Mike and I shoot some hoops in the barn?" J.J. asked.

"Sure, just be careful walking through the old stalls. They haven't been cleaned out since before your grandfather died ten years ago," she said sadly.

"I sure wish I could remember more about Grandpa. Mom says I was only two when he died."

Grams nodded and sighed, "That's right. Now, off you go."

They walked around the end of the house where the one-car, attached garage stuck out. They passed two large out buildings on their way to the barn, some thirty yards behind the house. The building on the left was nearly square. It looked like a one-car garage with a five-foot–wide storage area on each side. It was open at each end. The sliding doors had quit working long ago. The building on the right was long and narrow.

It was thirty, maybe forty, feet long and about fifteen feet wide. It had been used mainly for storage of farm implements.

When they got to the barn, Mike opened the door. J.J. stepped inside and turned on his flashlight. "Leave the door open, Mike."

Mike did so and stepped inside, turning his flashlight on also. Carefully they made their way through the narrow aisle with stalls on either side of them. Finally they got to the large open area of the barn where the tractors used to be parked.

Mike opened the double doors and the sunlight came streaming in. With the doors open, he could see the orchard where another old building sat abandoned. "Hey, why don't we go explore that old building over there?" Mike asked sarcastically as he got the doors opened.

"Let's do that another day. We'll need to talk with Grams about that first. Both Great-grandpa and Grandpa used to keep bees out there. I'm sure some of the old beehives are still there. I want to be sure there aren't a lot of bees still living out there."

"I see the basketball right where we left it the last time we were here. It's in the corner near the basket," Mike said as he went to get it. The boys had put up a hoop at the east end of the open area. They had spent many hours here shooting hoops and playing "H-O-R-S-E" and many other games.

Once he had the basketball, J.J. surprised him by saying, "Let's sit down first right in the center of the court."

Both boys were extremely startled when a blood-curdling scream tore through the old barn. They were frozen for a few seconds, especially Mike, who was still on edge after the dark-basement episode. Then a loud laugh came from back where the stalls were. "Ha-ha! I sure got you guys!" Jerry said, and laughed as he hustled out of the barn on a dead run. He didn't want the two boys to catch him before he could get to the house where Mom was.

"That little brat," snorted J.J. "It's a good thing he ran off! I'd clobber him if he were still here."

"So, how do you like a taste of your own medicine? He's just having fun. Forget it. Why did you want to sit on the floor in the middle of the basketball court?"

"I changed my mind. And especially since Jerry won't bother us again. I want to see what's inside that envelope."

"Open it up then."

J.J. carefully pulled the letter from the deep pocket on the front of his cargo pants. He slowly opened the envelope and found several papers inside. There were words on them written in a very neat script. J.J. began to read:

Dear First Great-grandson:

My name is Rolland Jacob Jamison. I was a first son of a first son of a first son and thus was given a very special gift. Considering you are reading this, you must also be a first son of a first son of a first son. Then you are the only one this will work for. During my lifetime I was able to do some very remarkable things. However, they had to be kept a secret that only I could know. You will be required to do the same should you decide to pursue and use the gift I am leaving for you. Think about it for a few minutes. If you are willing to accept the challenge this gift will present to you, then read on.

The two boys just stared at each other. "Are you really a first son of a first son of a first son?" Mike asked.

"I'm pretty sure Grandpa was a first son. I know my dad was Grandpa Jamison's first son. And I am my dad's first son. So, yes, I think I am."

"So what do you think of this letter and this challenge?"

"You know me. I like mysteries. So I think I'll keep reading and see where it leads." J.J. slowly turned the paper over and started reading again:

Congratulations. There is a box hidden in the basement of the house I used to live in. I built that house and made a special place to leave this gift when I felt the time was right. I'm now 72 years old and must be sure this gift is put away safely for the next recipient to find and use.

Once you get into the basement, make a left turn. Take four or five steps and you will come to a four foot by three foot opening in the wall on your left. This leads to the room where I dug the hole for the pump when we had the well drilled. You must enter this room, but be careful because it has a dirt floor and a hole in the center around the pump. I imagine the light in there won't work by the time you read this. So take a flashlight.

Once in the room, which has a low ceiling, go to the northwest corner on your left. Oh, by the way, take along or get from the basement a hammer and some sort of chisel. Count up seven bricks from the floor on the north wall right next to the corner. Then go east two bricks. Use the hammer and chisel and remove that *brick. You will find the box hidden behind the brick you removed. Good Luck.*

"Now that's some letter!" exclaimed Mike. "Are you going to do it? Are you going back into that dark old basement again?"

"Sure," replied J.J. with confidence. "I had fun the first time. Want to come along?"

"Sure. I'll hold the flashlight for you. That way it will not get totally dark on me again."

J.J. put the letter back in the envelope and slowly put it in his pocket.

2

"Let's hurry. I think we still have time before Mom calls us to go home," J.J. stated emphatically.

"I'm right behind you, and it's going to stay that way!"

They closed the double barn doors as well as the door on the front of the barn and raced back to the farmhouse. Once at the bottom of the stairs, J.J. walked into the main room and pulled the string hanging from the light fixture where the naked bulb was. He then located a hammer and chisel. Many of his grandfather's tools were still there on the workbench.

"I'm ready to go in now," he announced.

"I'm ready to watch from out here," came the reply. Mike wanted no part of the room with the well in it. Besides, he was too tall to fit in there.

J.J. cautiously climbed through the tight opening. *It's nearly pitch-black in here,* he thought to himself. He aimed the flashlight first at the floor and then at the ceiling. He did not want to trip over anything on the floor or bump his head on the ceiling. He would have to bend over just a little as well as watch where he stepped. There were bricks and debris all over the floor. At least he could get to the northwest corner without crossing the entire room.

"Mike, shine your light on the floor for me, and I'll shine my light on the wall and the ceiling."

"Okay, but this is as far as I'm coming," he replied with a shudder.

When he got to the corner, he counted up seven bricks on the north wall and then counted over two bricks to the east. Next he went to work with the hammer and chisel. Once he got the mortar chipped away, the brick came out easily.

"I've got the brick out and I can see the box inside the opening. I really do not want to put my hand in there, so I'll try to use the claw on the hammer to get it out." After several unsuccessful attempts, he announced, "It's no use. I'll have to reach in there."

"Don't you dare scream," said Mike. "I've had enough of your shenanigans for one day."

J.J. reached in and quickly pulled out the small rectangular box. "Ah! Ouch! Ouch! My hand is stuck!"

"You can't fool me again. Come on. Get over here so we can get out of here."

"Okay, I've got the box." He gingerly put the brick he had removed back into its place in the wall. "Now we can go upstairs. Shine your light on the floor in front of me so I can see to get back to the doorway." It didn't take long before the tools were back on the workbench and J.J. and Mike were up the stairs and standing in the yard. They were both breathing heavily.

"I'm glad to be out of the basement," said Mike in relief.

"It's over now. We've got the box. Let's see what's inside."

Then Mom's voice called out, "It's time to go home." She was standing in the doorway. Luckily J.J. had put the box in the same pocket of his pants as the letter.

"Okay, Mom. We're ready."

"Come in and say good-bye to Grams before we go. She's still in the front room talking with your brother."

Both J.J. and Mike went in to say good-bye to Grams. She was like a grandmother to Mike, too.

"Bye, Grams," J.J. said as he leaned over and kissed her on the cheek.

"Bye from me, too," echoed Mike.

"Good-bye, boys. You come back again real soon. I always like to see you both." She had that same knowing smile on her face.

On the ride back to town Mom asked the boys if they were hungry. When aren't a second-grade boy and two sixth-grade boys hungry? "Can we get a pizza?" Jerry asked.

"Pizza sounds real good," commented J.J.

"Mike, would you like to come over for some pizza?" Mrs. Jamison inquired.

"Sorry, Mrs. Jamison. I promised my mom I'd be home by six o'clock. She has a meeting at church to go to at six thirty, and she said she would have supper ready."

"J.J., want to come over tomorrow at two and study for the Civil War test?"

"Okay. I don't have anything planned for tomorrow."

"See you then."

"We'll have pizza with you another time," Mrs. Jamison added. She dropped Mike off at his place and then used her cell phone to order the pizza. They told her it would be delivered in twenty minutes.

As soon as he got home, J.J. went to his room and hid the box on the top shelf of his closet behind a larger box. Then he went downstairs to wait for the pizza. It arrived just as he was sitting down at the table.

They talked a little about the visit to Grams' while they ate the pizza. Both Jerry and J.J. loved pizza. Mom would eat it, but it wasn't her favorite food by far.

It was nearly seven thirty when they finished supper and dessert. Mom had baked cookies earlier and both boys loved her snickerdoodles.

"J.J., will you play a game of chess with me?" asked Jerry.

"Sure, but only one game. I'm really tired. You set up the board."

"Okay," Jerry said, enthusiastically. When the board was set up, he put a white pawn in one hand and a black pawn in the other. He switched them around behind his back and then held out both hands with the pieces hidden from view. "Pick one."

J.J. wanted the one in Jerry's left hand.

"You get black, so I get to move first." Jerry liked the black pieces better, but white had a big advantage in moving first. J.J. played better than Jerry, but Jerry would always learn something every time they played. This was how he improved. Neither boy played chess as well as Mike did. Mike was a champion!

J.J. relented and played two games with Jerry. By the time they finished it was just after nine thirty. That was Jerry's bedtime. J.J. was so tired he headed for bed also.

"Good night, Mom," said a weary J.J. It had been a long day.

"Good night from me too, Mom. Come up and tuck me in soon," Jerry added with a yawn.

"Good night, boys. I'll be up in a few minutes, Jerry."

3

J.J. HAD EVERY INTENTION OF GETTING THE BOX DOWN AFTER SUP-
per and opening it. However, he was really tired
when he sat down on his bed.

It can wait until morning, he thought. Quickly he got
out of his clothes and into his pajamas. He brushed his
teeth and went to bed. He went right to sleep.

J.J. awoke at six a.m. with a start. Suddenly wide
awake, he didn't know if some noise had startled him
or what. All he could think about was the box in his
closet. The first thing he did was to lock his bedroom
door. Then he got the box down and put it on his bed.
Slowly he opened it.

"Oh no," he moaned. "It's just another letter." Sure
enough there was a plastic bag containing some paper. There was a sheet with writing on it and another
with a map drawn on it. *This is a map of the back forty
around Grams' house,* J.J. thought to himself. *I've been to
that swimming hole before.* After looking at the map, he
concentrated on the letter. It read:

18

Dear Great-grandson,

Congratulations! You have reached step two in your quest for the special gift I have left for you. There is only one more step before your adventure begins. Now you must find the actual gift. Use the map I've included. If you have ever visited my place or listened to stories about my life and my son's life (your grandfather), you will recognize the farm and the back forty (acres). Take a shovel and go back to the creek directly behind Aunt Martha's old house. It is a little over a quarter of a mile back to the creek. You might want to take along some water and a towel. What you seek is buried three feet in the ground and is contained within a metal box. Everything will be explained when you open that box.

Sincerely,
Great-grandpa Jamison

Here we go again, thought J.J. *It's just another treasure hunt. I can't imagine what might be hidden out there from so long ago. Although he did go to a lot of work writing these letters and it took some planning to make the hiding place in the bricks in the basement. Digging a three-foot–deep hole is hard work, too. So there might be something to this little game he has me playing.*

Then J.J. looked back at the map again. He thought it would be easy to find the place that indicated where the box was hidden. He decided he would take the letter and the map over to Mike's house and talk with him about it.

It was very early Sunday morning, so J.J. had to make his own breakfast. No one was up, so he made himself a bowl of cereal, poured a glass of orange juice, and went out to the table on the porch to relax and eat. The world was so peaceful and quiet this early on a weekend morning.

At times like this he liked to either just sit and think or just read. This morning he thought while he ate. He wondered what it was that his great-grandfather had gone to so much work to preserve just for him.

He awoke with surprise when he heard, "Good morning, sleepyhead." His mom had come out onto the porch with her breakfast, too.

"What time is it, Mom?" The sun was way up in the eastern sky.

"It's nine fifteen. How long have you been out here?"

"I came out about six thirty with my breakfast. I guess I ate because my bowl is empty. I must have dozed off. I'd better start getting ready if we're going to church today."

"You have plenty of time. Church doesn't start until eleven o'clock. I got Jerry up before I came out here. We'll all be ready on time. I want to leave at ten forty."

J.J. took his dishes into the house and put them into the dishwasher. Then he went upstairs to get ready for church. He had to shower and change clothes.

He had a hard time paying attention in church. The minister was a good speaker, but today J.J. was thinking about the map he had found. He wanted to get over to Mike's house and show it to him.

Finally church was over. Mom decided to stop and get some fried chicken for lunch. He was glad because lunchtime would go faster if Mom did not have to cook first. They had a nice discussion while eating around the dining room table. Jerry asked if he could have a friend over, and J.J. asked if he could walk over to Mike's for a while. "There's a Civil War test on Tuesday, and we want to study together for it," he added.

At two o'clock J.J. walked through the backyards behind his house heading for Mike's place. Mike lived on the street right behind J.J.'s house and four houses east, closer to town. They both lived just a couple of blocks from the edge of town.

When he arrived he could hear Mike say, "Queen to King's Knight seven—checkmate."

"Darn!" exclaimed Daryl, Mike's eleventh-grade brother. "You beat me again. Why can't I ever beat you at this game?"

"You just have to play a little slower and think about your moves a little more. You might want to concentrate a little more on defense. You have improved a lot since you started playing just last year. It takes time to get better. Remember, I've been playing chess for five years." Mike had joined the chess club in second grade and had gone to weekly meetings ever since. The instructor was a teacher at the school. He was a grand master. So he taught them chess as well as letting them play games against each other.

"I know. But I just get so impatient at times. Thanks for helping me learn so much. I'll keep trying."

"Hi, guys," called out J.J. as he came up the steps to the big front porch. "Did you have a good game?"

"Sure," replied Daryl. "I lost again, but I hope I am learning something every time we play."

"Mike, are you ready to study a little for the Civil War test on Tuesday?" J.J. wondered.

"Sure. Let me get my notes."

"I brought along my textbook and the study sheet Dr. M gave us."

"You guys have a good study session," Daryl said

as he got up to leave. "I have some reading that needs to be done for school, too. I think I'll read out on the back porch." Daryl shut the front door as he went into the house.

Mike could hardly wait for Daryl to leave. "Well?" he asked. "What did you find in the box?"

"You'll never guess," J.J. answered with lots of sarcasm in his voice.

"How about another letter?"

"Wow! You are sharp. You guessed it. I found two things and one was another letter from my great-grandfather." And then he hesitated.

"Go on. What was the other?"

"A map of the old forty."

"Oh no. Does this mean another treasure hunt? I think your great-grandfather is playing a joke on you."

"I thought that at first, but then I thought about it for a while. Why would he go to all the work he did just for a joke? Here, take a look at the map."

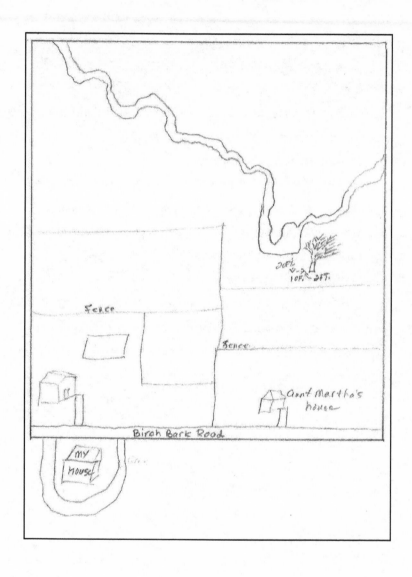

"Didn't we swim in that spot last summer?"

"We sure did. We even took Jerry along once. That means everything is still nearly the same as when Great-grandpa lived there."

"It should be easy to find that spot, then."

"Yes, it should. There's supposed to be a metal box buried about three feet deep there. The letter says to take a shovel, some water, and a towel. It could be hard work digging three feet down."

"When can we go?"

"So you really want to go?"

"Sure. At least it's something different to do besides homework and cleaning my room. And it won't be dark and dusty at the creek."

"That's right. I'll ask Mom tonight if we can go next Saturday. I'll tell her I can't wait to show Grams the old family Bible and ask her about it. I wanted to check with you first to see if you wanted to go, too."

"Of course I want to go. I don't want to be left out now. Especially after all the fun we had in the basement," he added with his own sarcasm.

"Did the letter say anything more about what was buried?"

"No. It only said that everything would be explained after we'd dug up the metal box."

"He must have put it in a metal box to protect it better," Mike added.

"That was my thought, too. It's been buried for a

long time."

"When did your great-grandfather die?"

"Well, he was seventy-two when he wrote the first note that started all of this. Mom has a family Bible where she records family births and deaths. I'll look it up when I get home. Now let's get into this Civil War stuff. I think it's interesting."

"Me, too," chimed in Mike. "If we work hard, the test on Tuesday should be easy."

So for the next couple of hours they looked over the study sheets and asked each other questions.

4

THE STUDYING REALLY PAID OFF FOR THE BOYS. WHEN THEY talked after school on Tuesday, they were sure they had known all the answers to all of the questions.

"I'm sure glad we studied together," Mike exclaimed happily.

"Me, too. We make a good team even if we are cousins!" J.J. came back.

"Don't get personal now."

The next day at lunch one of J.J.'s friends, Henrietta, was sitting alone getting ready to eat. She, J.J., and Mike have the same sixth-grade teacher, Dr. M. They are also all friends. Henri is a tomboy. She doesn't like dresses or nice shoes. Wearing shorts, a pullover shirt, and tennis shoes is her favorite mode of dress. Her hair is a light brown and cut in a short but cute style. Nearly everyone knows and likes Henri, as she is called. She is outgoing and willing to help anyone in need. Good grades come easily for her, but still she studies hard and always wants to learn something new. She is tall for her age, like Mike. She doesn't really like boys, but she tolerates them. Her somewhat oblong face is accented by striking, bright hazel eyes. Her ready smile and pleasant, positive attitude are contagious.

"Hi, Henri," called out J.J. as he walked past her to go sit with Mike and Tom.

"Hi, yourself," replied Henri. "Oh, here comes Erika. Hey, Erika, over here. I've saved a seat for you."

"Oh, hi, Henri. Thanks. I have to buy milk. I'll be right back."

"Okay."

When Erika got back, the girls chatted about how their morning had gone.

Erika is Henri's best friend. She is very quiet and of average size for a sixth-grader. She is all girl. Blond hair and brilliant blue eyes make her a standout. She does not like the attention she gets. She does like to wear nice clothes but does not overdo it. Grades and success in school come from her hard work. She is usually the top scorer on tests and has a fantastic memory. However she has to study hard to maintain the high level of performance she demands of herself. She is left-handed, with beautiful penmanship. Writing is a passion of hers and she hopes to be an author someday.

"Boy, this place sure is noisy," Erika said in a loud voice. "Why can't the aides keep it quieter in here?"

"Erika, there must be over a hundred kids in here and the floors are tile. There's nothing to absorb the sound. Anyway, this is a nice place to get to talk and not have to whisper like in the classroom."

"Yes, I guess you're right."

"Would you like to get together this Saturday and just hang out?" asked Erika.

"I'd love to, but my mom told me she was planning something special for me for Friday night and most of Saturday. How about we get together at my house around three o'clock on Sunday?"

"That would be perfect."

The girls finished their lunches, and they still had fifteen minutes of lunchtime left. They had to exit the lunchroom to make room for more kids to come in and eat. Most of the kids went out to the playground. There were tables and benches in shaded areas for those who just wanted to sit and talk. Most of the boys either played basketball or kickball. A few played soccer. The girls sat and talked.

When lunchtime was over, one of the duty aides would blow her whistle. That meant the kids should walk to the building and line up by classrooms in their designated areas. Talking was allowed in line until the teachers took their classes inside the building. Then silence was necessary.

J.J., Mike, and Henri all were in Dr. Emory's line. They walked into his room quietly with the other twenty-six students.

"Good afternoon, class," an exuberant Dr. M greeted them as they entered his classroom. Some of the students he greeted by name. "I have some really good news. There are only two and one-half hours of school left until the weekend."

"Yeah," said Billy. "I can hardly wait."

"Me, too," added Mary. "I get to visit my aunt at the lake tomorrow and spend the night."

Dr. M, as he allowed the students to call him, usually gave the students three or four minutes to get drinks, cool off, and settle down after lunch. Then it was time to get to work. He usually had something interesting to say or do to get the class started on a positive note.

Dr. Emory has taught in the Millville Public School for the past five years. The entire time has been spent in sixth grade. He is very popular with the students. He maintains strict classroom control but lets the students have fun at the same time. His students always seem to excel. Other teachers often asked him his secret, but he would just smile and say, "I guess I'm just lucky. I seem to get really good kids and they like to work for me." Actually being the only male teacher at the grade level meant that the principal often put the biggest troublemaking boy in his class. Sometimes if there were two, he got them both. That didn't seem to make any difference. Dr. M was still able to get through to them, too.

There's another aspect of Dr. M's work. Usually once a year he was called away by the government for a week or so. No one knew where he went or what he did. A special contingent from Washington, D.C., came and met privately with the school board. They made some kind of deal because the school board gave Dr. M time off whenever Major Stromberg called. The substitute was paid for by a fund administered by Major Stromberg. The school district could also dock Dr. M's salary for the time he was away. The government paid Dr. M very well for the work he did for them.

Dr. M has worked for the government nearly as long as he has been teaching in Millville. His government work started two years after coming to Millville. Because his students continued to outperform the other classes, he was able to be away occasionally and still successfully accomplish the goals set for his students.

Dr. Emory is a UFO specialist. He is called away to investigate strange UFO sightings or to collect unusual materials found near UFO sightings around the world. He works under the command of Major William Stromberg at the Department of Defense.

His findings and conclusions are all highly classified. They are kept safe and secure in a secret underground base in New Mexico.

Dr. M designated some of the money paid to him by the government to be used in his classroom. That's how the "cabin" came into being.

Today Dr. M was talking about the earthquake that just occurred around Washington, D.C. It measured 5.9 on the Richter scale. That made it a significant quake.

"Has anyone here ever been in an earthquake?" he asked. No one raised a hand. "I thought not. We don't have many earthquakes around here. I've recorded a little of the news to show you what it was like. But there is no way to explain it to you. It's an experience you must feel to understand how scary it is!"

He let the students watch about four minutes of the recorded quake news. It even showed some cracks in the Washington Monument.

"I'd just as soon not experience that," commented Jill.

"Me, too. That really looks scary," added Tim.

"Any more comments?" Dr. M asked. When there were none, Dr. M asked everyone to take out their math homework. They went over the methods used to find the answers. Then they traded papers, signed their names as checkers with a red pen, and proceeded to give the answers as Dr. M called on different students. He paid close attention while grading was taking place. It had to be done correctly, as the grades were important to each student. Dr. M asked each student to mark the number wrong at the top of the paper they checked. Then after the papers were returned to their owners and they had a couple of minutes to look them over, Dr. M asked for them to be collected by someone at each table. Then Dr. M came around and got each group of papers. He usually spot-checked the papers before recording the marks into his grade book.

5

THE NEXT HOUR WENT BY QUICKLY AS THEY DISCUSSED AND read some more about the Civil War. Finally the students' favorite time arrived. Two o'clock was the start of SSR. This was sustained silent reading. It lasted twenty-five minutes and occurred almost every day. Once in a while Dr. M even let it last five minutes extra.

"These are the students I have selected to read in the cabin today: Billy, Sarah, Mike, and Mary. You may get your books and climb up into the cabin."

"Yeah!" remarked a very happy Billy. "I haven't been in the cabin for several weeks."

"Me, either!" exclaimed Mary. "I've been hoping to get picked again."

Only four students were selected each day during SSR time to read up there. Dr. M kept track of who read there and how often they had been selected. He tried to give everyone a turn.

The cabin was a special place in Dr. M's classroom.

The cabin was a platform that had been built up three feet off the floor, and the students really liked to read up there.

To get into the cabin, the kids had to climb up the steps. There was a hand railing for safety. Since Dr. M's classroom had a ten-foot ceiling, the students could stand up in the cabin. The floor was reinforced to hold the weight of the four students reading there.

There were doors on the lower part so that underneath the cabin was usable storage space. There was also a railing along the front of the edge of the cabin. This allowed the students to be visible from the classroom. It was also for safety. No one was ever allowed to climb through this railing to get into or out of the cabin.

There were four beanbag chairs in the cabin. The kids could take their water bottles if they had them.

Also in the cabin was a short, narrow rectangular table. On this table were an old-fashioned wooden locomotive and six cars. These were just for use during SSR. Dr. M had made the train from special wood supposedly shipped in from a missionary friend in Africa. The wood was unlike any other in the world. It was very heavy. It could have come from some other world.

There was some kind of light inside each train car. "That's what makes them glow all the time," Dr. M answered when asked about his train. "At least it gets the kids' attention."

When the students entered the cabin to read, they would first get comfortable on the beanbag chairs. Then as they would start to read, they would place one hand on one of the train cars and keep it there until they'd read at least one paragraph.

The strange thing is that the time seemed to pass very quickly for those reading in the cabin. Could the train have special powers? Many of the students at least pretended that it did. They said it helped them concentrate more. It helped them really get into their reading.

"I just started reading a minute ago," Bobby said yesterday when SSR ended.

"Me, too," reported Sue.

They had actually been reading for nearly thirty minutes. "I remember everything like I was actually there," Jim reported from yesterday also. "I did not want to stop reading."

Beth, who was not reading in the cabin, got angry about halfway through SSR time. Her angry whisper could be heard all over the room. "Stop it, Larry! Quit it!"

"Shush," answered Larry in a worried whisper. "Dr. M will hear you."

"He sure will," came the firm but soft voice of Dr. M, who was suddenly standing right above Larry. He had a stern look on his face. "If you poke her again, you will clean the entire floor before you leave today."

Dr. M had been known to ask each student to throw a piece of trashed paper onto the floor at the end of the day for a troublemaker to have some cleaning up to do.

"Ah, okay. Sure, Dr. M. I was just foolin' around. Sorry," came the meek reply from Larry.

"Thank you," Dr. M said, moving back toward the center of the room.

Dr. M noticed that Matt did not have a book to read. Matt had three choices. He could write sentences using his spelling and vocabulary words. He could read in his social studies book. Or he could visit the classroom library.

A classroom library of over three hundred books was kept by Dr. M. Many of them were Accelerated Reader, or AR, books. The others could just be read for a day or could be borrowed and used for a book report. AR books could also be used for book reports. Students had to do one book report every grading period.

6

SR TIME WAS ALSO WHEN THE STUDENTS WORKED ON THEIR AR program. This was a graduated program that was run on the computer. Each student in grades two through six took part in it.

When the school year started, each student would take a computer reading test to determine their AR level. This reading level would have a range like 4.0 to 4.9 or 5.0 to 5.9. The computer checked the test and printed out the results. The teacher filed this result in each student's AR folder.

The library was dedicated to the AR program. So the media specialist had ordered hundreds of books and computer tests for the AR program. The books on the shelves would have an AR level taped to their spines. Thus the kids could easily find AR books. The reading score was written on the inside cover of the book. The media center was open at lunchtime for students with passes as well as for twenty minutes after school, Monday through Thursday. On Fridays the media center closed when school was out at three o'clock.

The students went to the media center to take a test after reading a book. The tests were all multiple choice and the computer instantly checked the test and printed out the results. The student had to score 70 percent or better to earn points. Each book was assigned points based on its length and level of difficulty within its AR level. Tests could not be retaken. So students often reviewed a book before they took the test. Books were worth from half a point to ten points.

The teacher and the student would set the number of points that student needed to reach during the grading period. The total number of points would then decide what the grade would be for AR reading. It was up to the student whether he wanted an A, B, or C in reading.

Dr. M's classroom was a very special place. He did not use the overhead lights. Instead he had six torchiere-type pole lamps spread around the room. He also had a lamp on his desk and one up in the cabin.

At first glance, the room appeared somewhat dark. However, after spending a few minutes in the room, your eyes adjusted and you could see and read without any eye strain. A few parents had to decide for themselves about the lamps. So they stopped by. After a few minutes they were convinced and became supporters.

Dr. M finally announced, "Time to finish the page you are reading and mark your place. Everyone be back in your seats in three minutes." His voice penetrated into all corners of the room.

Dr. M has a big black cow bell with bright orange flames that had been painted on by his son. Today he walked over and rang it. *"Clankity, clank, clank,"* it sounded. It was time to stop reading. The students needed the loud noise to get them out of their books and back into the classroom. Surprisingly this almost always happened to the people reading in the cabin. There was something special at work here that could not be explained.

When the students were back in their seats, Dr. M spoke again: "Okay, let's review what we covered in class today." He would spend fifteen to twenty minutes every day asking questions and sort of reteaching everything they should have learned that day. Then came, "Any questions?" Finally Dr. M commanded, "Pick up all the papers and pencils that have fallen onto the floor. Then you can pack up and get ready to go home."

As the students left the classroom, Dr. M was right there at the door. "Good night," he said. "Have a great weekend!"

7

A<small>S ANOTHER WEEK CAME TO AN END, THE STUDENTS WERE</small> busy talking about what they were going to do on the weekend. Nearly everyone had some sort of plans.

Erika met Henri by the front door of the school after the bell rang. They were walking the six blocks to Deano's. Deano's was a favorite hangout for the kids after school and on weekends.

A few kids were there when they arrived. Some parents were able to pick their kids up at school and drop them off at Deano's place.

Erika and Henri found an empty booth just as a soda clerk came up to them. "What can I get for you two ladies today?" he asked with a smile.

"Hi, Hank. I'll have a strawberry soda," said Henri.

"Make that two," chimed in Erika.

As they sat there an unusual thought came into Henri's mind. "How did you come to live here in Millville?" she asked Erika.

"Well, my parents wanted to live in a small town. So when my dad found a job here, we moved from Detroit. That was when I was in third grade. I didn't like this small town at first. Then I met you and now I'm happy and have adjusted."

"You're a good friend, Erika. My parents were the same way. They wanted a small town, too. We moved here when I was in kindergarten. It was hard for me at first, too, but I was so young and everyone at school was friendly. The neighbors were also wonderful."

"Don't forget I'm coming over on Sunday at three o'clock. What should we do?"

"Let's not plan anything. We'll just see what happens."

"Okay. Well, I've got to go," Henri added. "I need to get home to see what surprise Mom has ready for me. I'll be busy tonight and all day Saturday."

Henri quickly walked home. It was only six more blocks from Deano's. Erika had walked the first two with her and then turned north to go to her place.

When Henri got into the kitchen, there was a message on the island for her. It was written by her mother and relayed a telephone message from her Gramma Tessie. Gramma Tessie was Henri's mother's mother, and she lived alone about a mile and a half north of town. Her house was about thirty yards up a slight incline from a small but beautiful lake.

Gramma Tessie lived alone because she had lost her

husband, Harold, to cancer about four years ago. She is sixty-three years old, still drives, and is in very good health. She and J.J.'s grandmother (Grams) are good friends.

The message read:

Dear Henri,

Gramma Tessie would like you to come out this evening and spend the night with her. She will be in to pick you up at six o'clock. You will drive back to her place for a homemade supper.

The note went on to explain that Tessie would bring her home Saturday afternoon. The note was signed by Henri's mom. There was a postscript to the note explaining that Gramma Tessie had something she wanted to talk with Henri about.

Henri needed to get busy as it already was nearing five o'clock. Gramma would be arriving in an hour.

What could Gramma want to talk with me about? Henri wondered to herself. She could think of nothing. However, Henri really liked her and they usually spoke on the phone every weekend. They had become especially close three years ago, when Henri's father mysteriously disappeared. She had been nine at the time. Gramma Tessie helped her and her mom get through that very tough time.

Learning to swim at Gramma Tessie's was one of Henri's favorite memories from her lake visits. There was a raft about twenty yards out into the lake. The water was about three feet deep at the end of the dock where Tessie kept her rowboat. At the raft the water was six feet deep. She could dive in from the dock and with five or six strokes make it to the raft and climb on. She never did this alone even after she learned how to swim. There was a ladder attached to the raft, so climbing on was easy.

Many times she and Erika would ride their bikes out to Gramma's just to go for a swim. Henri decided to call Gramma to be sure things were still on for tonight.

"Hi, Gramma," she said when Gramma Tessie answered on the third ring.

Gramma Tessie had a very cheery voice. "Is everything okay, dear? Can you still come out tonight?" Her gramma sounded worried.

"Sure. Everything is just fine. I just wanted to be sure you were still coming to get me."

"I'll be there in an hour. Will you be ready?"

"I sure will. What will we be doing?"

"Just having supper. Plus I have something to show you. It's a bit of a surprise."

"Okay. I'll be ready at six o'clock. See you then. Good-bye, Gramma."

"Good-bye, dear."

Henri quickly packed a few things and then read a couple of chapters in her book while she waited. She had to write a report for English, and this book was part of it. It wasn't due for a couple of weeks, but she wanted to get the book read to be sure she met the deadline. So far after seventy-five pages her book was pretty good. It was a mystery about a small town where a young boy and girl had saved many lives.

Finally six o'clock arrived as did Gramma Tessie. She was right on time, as usual. Henri raced out the front door as the big black Tahoe pulled into the driveway. Henry had left her mom a note on the kitchen island telling her that she had been picked up by Gramma Tessie.

"Hi, Henrietta," called Gramma Tessie through the rolled-down window. She had always called her Henrietta. No nicknames for Gramma Tessie.

"Hi, Gramma," called back Henri. As she entered the big SUV she continued, "I'm really excited. When will you show me the surprise?"

"Later. After supper will be soon enough. It can wait even if you can't."

"Okay," came the reply along with a long exaggerated sigh of impatience. "I know there's no getting you to change your mind. What's for supper?"

"We'll have homemade spaghetti and meatballs. It's all ready to heat up. Plus there's fresh chocolate cake for dessert," came the response along with a disarming smile.

"That sounds good, Gramma." This time there was genuine enthusiasm in her voice. She liked Gramma's meatballs, and chocolate cake was her all-time favorite. This was going to be a very good visit.

After supper was finished, Gramma suggested they take a walk down to the lake. Gramma had her bag hanging from her shoulder and Henri wondered if her surprise was inside.

When they got to the dock, Gramma surprised her. "We'll be taking the boat out in the morning. It will be better then, as it is getting too dark tonight." She surprised her again by asking, "Henrietta, what do you remember about your father?"

"Well," she replied after a few seconds, "I was only nine when he disappeared." She paused again and then went on hesitantly. "I honestly don't remember a lot. I think he had a deep voice and was tall. Of course nearly everyone is tall to a nine-year-old. I remember him pushing me on a swing and trying to teach me to float in a swimming pool. Mom always reminds me how much he loved me. She's convinced he would never just leave us. She thinks something bad must have happened to him. It seems so strange that both J.J.'s dad and my dad disappeared at the same time, doesn't it, Gramma?"

"Yes, it does, Henrietta, my dear. I can assure you that your father loved you very much. He would never have just left his family without a really good reason. I think that's enough for tonight. It's time to turn in. Breakfast will be at eight o'clock sharp and then a boat ride."

"What do you mean 'without a really good reason,' Gramma? And can't you tell me what the surprise is?"

"All in good time, my dear. All in good time. Everything in time is entwined together. We have to go at it piece by piece. Let's get back up to the house. There will be more answers in the morning."

Henri had a really hard time getting to sleep that night. She even left the window open and a slight breeze blew in from the lake. She wondered about the surprise. And she could not get Gramma's words about her father out of her head. There was more that she wanted, needed to know. Maybe Gramma Tessie would give her some answers in the morning. After a bit, sleep finally came to her.

She awoke to a bright sunny morning. After breakfast was finished and the dishes were in the dishwasher, they headed down to the lake.

"You'd better wear this hat, Henrietta. The sun is quite warm and it's very bright out on the lake. Do you have sunglasses?"

"Yes. I picked up the pair I keep in my room upstairs."

"Will you carry this picnic basket?"

"Sure," she replied as they headed down to the

dock. When they got there Henri saw two life preservers and two oars already in the boat. Gramma sure was prepared. She carefully placed the picnic basket into the small boat. Gramma stepped right into the boat and took a seat in the back facing forward. "Should I row?"

"Yesiree," replied Gramma with authority. "Let's get going. The sun has been up a couple of hours and it's already starting to get hot. Even though the temperature will only reach seventy today, it will feel much warmer out here on the lake."

Henri sat in the middle position in the boat facing back toward Gramma. Then she slowly rowed the boat away from the dock. She had to face away from the direction the boat was headed while she rowed. Gramma sat facing forward so she could see where they were going and direct Henri.

Henri knew how to row so she could easily follow Gramma's directions when a course change was needed.

"We're just going a little ways," Gramma explained. "Turn around a little to your right and you will see where two small patches of land jut out into the lake. We will need to head right between them. They looked to be at least forty feet apart and only about fifty yards ahead.

So Henri rowed and Gramma navigated. Soon they were approaching the shore exactly between the two points of land. A small sandy beach came into view as they neared the shore. There was even a picnic table there under a large oak tree.

"I don't remember this place," exclaimed Henri. "It's really nice. Look at that sandy beach and there's a place for our picnic."

Gramma responded, "I had it made about a month ago. It will be a perfect place for people to row to, swim, and have a picnic. Not many people know about it yet. I hope only people who live here on the lake will use it."

After they had pulled the boat ashore a little, they sat down at the picnic table.

"Henri," began Gramma Tessie in a very serious voice. "I want to tell you something that has been a secret for a very long time."

8

MIKE'S MOTHER HAD OFFERED TO DRIVE THE BOYS BACK out to Grandma Jamison's farm Saturday morning. So she pulled up in front of J.J.'s place about ten o'clock.

"Hi," called J.J. from the front porch. "Isn't it a beautiful day?"

"Hi, J.J. It sure is," replied Mrs. Hollywell. "Are you ready to go?"

"Sure thing. I even brought some bottles of water. Grams said she would make us some sandwiches for lunch. She'll also have some chips and canned pop for us. Where's Mike?"

"He wasn't quite ready. So I came over here to get you first. We'll swing back around the block and get him on the way. He'd better be ready by the time we get there!"

Fortunately Mike was standing on the front steps waiting when his mom stopped in front of the house. "I'm sure glad you are finally ready," she said with a smile.

"Sorry," Mike said sheepishly. "I just couldn't find my swimsuit. I thought we might take a dip in the old swimming hole. But I couldn't find it, so I gave up."

"I hope you guys have fun. After I drop you off I'm driving over to Freedville to see my sister. I plan to stay until around three or so. That means I'll be back here about four o'clock. Will you be okay for that long?"

"I'm sure we'll be okay, Mom."

It only took ten minutes to drive to the old farm. Grams came down the old brick steps and out to the dirt and grassy circle drive when Mrs. Hollywell and the boys drove up.

"I'll be back to get them at four o'clock. Is that okay?"

"It sure is. I'm sure they can keep busy around here doing something that's fun. I've got a lunch all planned for them. I thought they might like to take a picnic to the back forty."

Mike and J.J.'s eyes got large as they looked at each other. How could she know they had been planning to ask if they could walk to the old swimming hole on the back forty? It must just be a coincidence.

With that Mrs. Hollywell drove around the circle drive and came out onto Birch Bark Road. She turned left and continued on in the direction she had been traveling when she arrived at Gram's place. Freedville was only about twenty miles further west and a couple of miles south.

The boys followed Grams into the house and sat down in the front living room with her.

"How old was Great-grandpa Jamison when he died?" J.J. asked tentatively.

"Well, let's see. He was seventy-five when he died and that was seventeen years ago. Why do you ask?"

"Thanks, Grams. I was just wondering. Mike and I found an old family Bible in a trunk in the basement. It had Great-grandpa's initials on the cover. That got me to wondering about him. He built this house, didn't he?"

"Yes, he did. I'm surprised you knew that."

"I spend a lot of time out here so I should know something about the place," he tried to explain. "Did you know there were books in the trunk in the basement?"

"There are a lot of things in the boxes in the basement. I'm not surprised there are some old books there," Grams said wistfully. "What are you boys going to do first?"

"Let's put the croquet set up and play a few games," J.J. answered.

"That's a great idea. We used to have some real competitive games out there on the lawn when the family would get together. It sure was fun watching Uncle Jack drive someone into that deep ditch out by the road. He sure got a kick out of that!" Grams added with a bit of nostalgia in her voice. "Oh yeah, and my husband would get so upset with him for doing it, too. Oh, those were the good old days."

"Do you want to play, Grams?" ventured Mike.

"Oh dear, no," she replied. "I'm much too old and rickety for that. But I would love to sit on the front porch and watch you two play for a while. It will do me good."

The boys got the wickets pushed into the ground and Grams got three glasses of cold lemonade set up on the front porch. They must have played ten or eleven games before they decided to quit. They were evenly matched and each won a few games. And because the ground had some uneven spots in it, there was some luck involved also.

The boys came up to sit with Grams on the porch. "This lemonade sure hits the spot. It's probably only seventy-two degrees, but I'm hot," sighed Mike.

"You must be playing too hard," commented J.J. "What say we help Grams with that picnic lunch and head off to the back forty?"

"I have everything laid out on the counter in the kitchen except the meat, condiments, and the pop," Grams informed them. "I'll get those items out of the refrigerator and you can make your own sandwiches. There are some ziplock bags there for chips, sandwiches, and cookies."

"Cookies?" smiled J.J. happily. "Did you bake,

Grams?"

"Yes I did. I made four dozen peanut butter cookies early this morning. They came off the cooling racks just before you drove up."

With the lunch put into a backpack, which hung from Mike's shoulders, the boys went out the door and down the steps.

Grams went back into the house after wishing the boys a grand adventure. Again the boys' faces were aghast at her comment. Did she know?

J.J. took the lead and headed toward the back of the house in the opposite direction they had planned. "Why are we going this way?"

"Because we have to get a shovel. How do you think we are going to dig up that box?"

"Oh, I had forgotten that little detail."

"I think I once saw a small folding camp shovel in the garage. I think it will fit into your bag. Then Grams won't see it and ask us a lot of questions."

"Good idea. We can go around and go out the west driveway." After some searching in the garage, the boys found the camp shovel. "Here it is," Mike said. "And it does fit into my bag. Let's go."

"From what we learned from Grams, that letter from my great-grandpa was written twenty years ago," J.J. stated. "He only got it written just three years before he died."

The boys followed the circle drive around the west

side of the house. They crossed Birch Bark Road and headed east to Aunt Martha's old place. They went up her driveway and started north across the field. A friend of Grams lived in Aunt Martha's house now. It had been left to Grams when Aunt Martha died. She has been renting it to a friend who needed a place to stay and couldn't afford much rent. This person's car was gone so the boys knew no one was home.

The final leg of the adventure had begun.

9

IKE AND **J.J.** HAD TO WATCH THEIR STEPS AS THEY walked through the fields. There were large rocks and deep ruts to be wary of. One could easily turn an ankle stepping down wrong. It seemed like farther than a quarter of a mile as the boys climbed over the second fence.

"I'm sure glad no one raises cattle back here anymore. Grams tells about the time my grandpa tried to take a shortcut to the swimming hole by climbing over one of these fences. He thought the old farmer had taken his bull into the barn. Wrong! Gramma says Grandpa barely made it back to the fence and tumbled over when the bull came charging after him."

"I'd like to have seen that," Mike said.

"Yeah. Me, too," came J.J.'s thoughtful reply. "Looks like we're almost there. I can see the creek."

"Let's find that double bend where the swimming hole is."

"I think we're coming right up on it."

Sure enough they walked right up to the old swimming hole. "Did you bring the map?" asked Mike.

"Yes, I did, but I can remember the directions and the measurements. It's twenty feet from the bend that turns north. Then it's ten feet east. We dig two feet shy of the big tree if it is still there. They should both lead to the same spot.

"Oh, good. The tree is still there. This could have been a disaster if the tree had been gone. We both forgot to bring a tape measure!" continued J.J. with some surprise in his voice.

"I wonder why your great-grandfather forgot to mention that?" countered Mike.

"It might have been to see how resourceful we are. It doesn't matter. The tree's here and I think we can estimate two feet."

Mike measured three of his shoe lengths and announced, "Dig here." Mike got the shovel out of the backpack he had placed on the ground nearby. He began to dig. The ground was remarkably soft and within a few minutes he had a hole two feet deep and two feet across. "Your turn, J.J. You get to dig it up."

"Okay, here goes." J.J. continued the digging and soon the metallic clink of metal on metal sounded.

"That's it!" shouted Mike enthusiastically. "You've found it!"

"I think I have. We have. We're working together here."

J.J. carefully dug out around what appeared to be a metal box buried end wise deeper into the earth. He grabbed hold of the end with both hands and gently pulled. The box slowly came out of its very old grave. He wiped the box on the grass and saw no identifiable markings on the oblong box. It was about one inch tall, two inches wide, and ten inches long.

"Can you open it?" Mike asked as he sat down on the ground next to J.J.

"I'm trying." Finally he found a small seam and was able to get a fingernail into it. His fingernail wasn't strong enough, though.

"Here, try my knife," Mike suggested.

Carefully J.J. edged the blade into the opening. He pried just a little and the full length of the top popped up attached on the back by an inside hinge.

"What's in it?" Mike wondered.

"Guess what? It's another piece of paper inside a bag. What'd I tell you? Oh, wait. There's something else in the bag. It looks like it might be a bracelet of some sort." He carefully opened the bag and took out the paper. "Here, hold these, but be careful with them." Then he took out the bracelet.

"Is it really just a bracelet?"

"Yes, it's just a bracelet. It's wrapped in a second bag. It looks like it has a flat stone on top shaped like a rectangular watch. I think we better see what the papers say first."

Mike handed J.J. the papers. "It's your gift. You do the reading."

J.J. began to read the third letter from his great-grandfather.

Dear Great-grandson,

This is the final prize. Please be very careful with it. There is a special process you must go through to activate it. The stone is very powerful and must be used with great care and thought. Once you have activated it, it will work for you until you deactivate it. This is serious business, not to be entered into lightly.

J.J. and Mike just looked at each other. Was this a joke to scare them? Was J.J.'s great-grandfather just having fun with them? Or was this a serious matter?

"I don't know what to do," J.J. finally commented.

"I do," Mike stated emphatically. "Read the rest of the letter. It can't do any harm."

After thinking for a moment or so, J.J. answered. "You're right. I might as well see what it says this thing can do." And so he read on.

This bracelet has a very powerful stone in it that comes not from this earth. The stone is in the shape of your right-hand thumb. You will need to put your thumb onto the stone after you complete the activation process. It will burn a little when you press your thumb onto the stone, but it will not hurt you. You are the next rightful owner.

Here's how it works. When you press your thumb onto the stone, time will stop momentarily and then move backward exactly one hour. That one hour will be relived exactly as it happened unless you do something to cause it to change. You will be the only one who knows the last hour is being relived. Any changes you make or facilitate will be permanent and will remain unchangeable.

There is one more thing. There is another stone similar to yours but just a little different. If things work out as they always have in the past, you will be made aware of that gift and the person who has it when the proper time arrives. Do not go looking for it or the person who has it. Do not ask any questions about gifts or stones. And definitely do not mention your gift.

Now here is what you do to activate the stone.

You must place it in a pan of water and slowly bring it to a boil. If you press on the back of the stone through the strap, the stone will come loose. Heat it to a boil. The stone will start to glow. Dump the water out and place the stone on a cooling rack. After it cools enough to touch it, place it back into the strap. Then press your right thumb firmly onto the stone. It should just fit. As I said earlier, this procedure will burn your thumb a little, but no harm will come to your thumb or the stone. The stone will not be able to be removed from the strap unless you are ready to stop using it. Then you will need to put the stone in a freezer for 24 hours. The freezing will allow you to remove the stone from the strap. Then you must boil the stone again and follow the same procedure as before. Place your thumb onto the stone. It will burn again, but the power will be deactivated. Next press the stone back into the strap, and it will become dormant. Once you put the stone on, you are not to take it off.

Now you need to fill in the hole you dug and place the bracelet back into the bag. Put the bag and these *instructions into your pocket. When you get back to the farmhouse or wherever you are going, wait at least 24 hours before trying to activate the stone. That will give you time for all of this to settle into your mind.*

Sincerely,

Great-grandpa Jamison

"Well, that's quite a fairy tale," Mike finally commented. "Now I know your great-grandpa was having fun with us. Can you believe that guy? I bet he really enjoyed devising this little scheme."

"Yeah, I know. But thanks for helping me out with all of this. I'll put the bracelet back into the bag and put it and the letter into my pocket for the time being. Let's get this hole filled in. I think I'll keep the metal box and put it in Gram's basement."

"Here, I'll fill in the hole," volunteered Mike.

"Thanks. How about we sit in the shade on the other side of this tree and eat our lunch?" suggested J.J.

"That's a great idea. Suddenly I'm very hungry and thirsty."

"Me, too," said J.J. as he sat down on the ground in the shade. "This has been quite a week."

"What do you say we do something special next weekend to celebrate the end of all these treasure hunts?" suggested Mike.

"That's a great idea. I wonder if I should remind Grams about the family Bible we found in the basement last week? I told her about it when I asked about when Great-grandpa died. She didn't seem too interested in seeing it then."

"Then let's hold off mentioning it again so soon," Mike said. "I'll bet she doesn't remember that Bible. And that was where you found the letter addressed to you. She probably never opened it after he died. It just got put in with some of his other books. Besides she has her own Bible as well as that family Bible in her front living room."

"Yes," J.J. said thoughtfully. "I think I'll wait to get it to show her until the next time we're here. She might have some nice stories to tell us about some of the photos I saw in that old Bible."

"Wonderful," sighed Mike. "Another trip into that dark, dusty basement. And the trunk is way back in that far room where there's no light."

"Don't worry. We'll just make it a very fast in and out trip. I only want to get that one Bible. Think of what it might mean to Grams?"

After they had finished their lunch, the boys packed up and headed back. They both wished they had brought along swimsuits. It had gotten warm and a dip in the old swimming hole sure would have felt good. They weren't sure they had time to swim anyway. Mrs.

Hollywell was due back to pick them up soon.

Mike folded the shovel and placed it in his bag. Then they started back to the farmhouse. It didn't seem to take nearly as long to walk back home as it did to walk out there.

Grams was sitting on the front porch when they got back. "Did you have a good time?" she asked.

"Yes, Grams," J.J. answered. "Thanks for all the food. It sure tasted good. We drank everything we took and I'm still thirsty. I think I'll go inside and get a drink."

"Me, too," Mike added.

"It's quite nice here on the porch. I think I will sit out here a while longer," Grams said.

When they got inside Mike carefully took the shovel out. He went through the kitchen and the large pantry room and down the steps into the garage. He left the shovel on one of the old boxes still sitting in the garage. It was hard to believe that J.J.'s great-grandfather actually painted cars in this old place! At least that's what Grams had told them.

As the boys came back out onto the front porch, Mike's mom pulled into the driveway.

"Nice timing," Mike pointed out.

Neither of the boys wanted to answer any questions Grams might have. They might get their stories mixed up and she would find out about the bracelet. Little did they know how much Grams already knew about that special bracelet.

Mrs. Hollywell spent a few minutes talking with Grams and then they got into the car and headed home.

"Bye, come again," Grams called from the porch.

"Bye, Grams," the two boys chorused in unison.

10

As Henri looked at Gramma Tessie with much anticipation, she was a little apprehensive as well. *What could this be about?* she thought.

"The story starts a long time ago, before my lifetime. I can only trace it back three generations, but it goes back much farther than that. I first learned about the necklace from my mother just before she died, bless her soul. She was very hesitant to tell me as I remember. Here's what she told me:

"'Tessie, I was given a special necklace when I was fourteen. It was passed down to me from my great-grandmother. The ability to use the power of this necklace skips two generations. It is made available to the firstborn great-granddaughter.'

"Do you understand so far?"

"Sure," Henri said. "What's to understand? There's some special power that has been passed down in our family and it skips two generations each time. And I suppose I'm next, huh? You're kidding me, right?"

"Henrietta, I've never been more serious. There is more behind this than I can tell you or that you can understand right now. As you grow older you'll understand more and be able to make better use of this information. I assure you that what I am about to tell you is the absolute truth. It's up to you whether to believe it or not. However, you know me well enough to trust my judgment. And you know that I would never lie to you or do anything that would ever be harmful to you. Do you believe that at least?"

"That I believe. I love you and I do trust you. Please continue."

"Okay. Your great-grandmother was given a very special necklace by her great-grandmother. Actually it was passed down from her great-grandmother to her grandmother and finally to her. However, she was the only one who could use its power after her great-grandmother. The others were just caretakers. That's the way it was when it came to me. The necklace itself will tell you about the power it has. I do not know what it does except to stress that it is very powerful. The necklace is also very important to the future. That's all I know."

"So how do you know it works?" Henri wanted to know.

"I don't know if it works. I do know that my mother stressed its importance to me the way I am to you. You will have to follow the instructions it gives you and see where that leads you. My mother had these same instructions from her mother. And that brings us to you. It is now up to you to use its power for good."

"That's a lot to take in, Gramma. I'm only twelve years old. What can a twelve-year-old do?"

"Yes, I realize that. But you are a very mature twelve. I think you are ready to start learning about the necklace and its power. I've had a strange feeling when I've held the necklace for about two weeks now. It's been vibrating slightly. I have had a feeling something very big and important is about to happen. That has made me decide it is time you had it. It does not matter who you get it from. Your mom does not know about it. In my will it's written where I have kept the necklace, and I have specified that it should go to you upon my death. That would've ensured that you received it. Now that I'm giving the necklace to you while I'm alive, I'll have all mention of it removed from my will. Then the secret will be safe."

"Can you show me the necklace?"

"Yes, I can. It is right here in this blue bag." Gramma Tessie undid the drawstring on the brightly colored bag and took out a heart-shaped necklace on a leatherlike cord. "Here it is," she said as she held it up for Henri to see.

Carefully Henri touched the dark blue stone. "It

sparkles in the sun!" she exclaimed. "The strap looks very old. I can't tell what it is made of," she said as she touched it.

"The sparkle comes from inside the stone. I've never seen it sparkle before until you touched it. And I could never figure out what the strap was made from."

"May I hold it?"

"Sure. From now on it's yours until you are finished with it."

As Henri took it into her hands, she gave a start. "It does seem to have a faint vibration to it, and it's getting stronger."

"Perhaps it recognizes you. You are the next true wearer of the necklace."

"How do I find out how it works? I'm curious about what kind of power it has."

"All I can tell you is that you will be told what to do when you hold the necklace tightly in both hands in the dark. Then all will be revealed to you. That's the message my mom passed on to me to give to my first-born granddaughter."

"I guess that means we wait until tonight, then," Henri concluded. "Wait a minute," she suddenly interrupted. "Does this mean that you and Mom were the skipped generations?"

"Yes, that's right."

"So shouldn't you have given it to Mom to keep for me?"

"Yes, normally that's the way it would happen. But I think it was alerting me that it was time to pass it on to you.

"Finding out more about the necklace is something you must do alone. The necklace will tell you what to do. Just don't tell anyone that it has special powers or that you think it has special powers."

"Okay, what do we do now, Gramma?"

"Now we have a picnic. That's after you put the necklace around your neck and inside your shirt. You may also keep the bag. It was given to me with the necklace."

Henri tentatively put the necklace over her head and tucked it inside her shirt. The tingling she had felt went away. She hardly knew she was wearing the necklace.

"What did you bring for our picnic?" Henri asked.

"Turkey and egg salad sandwiches plus whole carrots. There's Jell-O for dessert and four bottles of water."

"Sounds wonderful." And they started to eat.

They ate lunch over the next half hour or so. They talked about family and Henri's school. The subject of the necklace did not come up again. It seemed that once Gramma had given her the necklace, she was out of the picture.

The picnic table was up the beach a little from the water. It was situated under a large oak tree. It was late spring so the tree was a beautiful shade of dark green.

There were several ducks swimming in the lake. There was almost no sound. They just sat there for a while enjoying the peacefulness of the lake.

Finally Gramma Tessie spoke. "I think it's time to get back to the house. It won't be long and I'll need to take you back home. Why don't you talk with your mom and come back out next weekend to swim. You could invite your friend Erika to come along and Joey and a friend would also be welcome."

"That's a great idea. I'll ask Mom about it as soon as I get home. Thanks, Gramma. And thanks for the necklace."

"You're welcome. Now that you have the necklace, let's not speak about it again. My job is done in that regard."

"Okay. Mum's the word. But don't you want to know if it works? Aren't you interested in what it does? I would be."

"It's better if I know nothing more about it. Do not ever tell anyone where you got it. There is another stone similar to this one. When the time is right, the person wearing it will be revealed to you. Do not look for this person or ask anyone about the stone in your necklace. Do not talk about this to anyone. You will soon have someone to talk with who has a power similar to yours."

"Wow! This is some mystery. I wonder what I'm getting myself into?" Henri added a little bit awestruck.

They picked up the picnic things and loaded them into the boat. Then Gramma climbed in. Finally Henri pushed the boat all the way into the water and jumped in. She situated herself in the middle of the boat and started to row out of the secluded cove.

As they rowed away, the branches parted ever so slightly from just behind where they had eaten lunch. Someone had overheard everything they had said.

At four o'clock Gramma drove Henri back home. She came inside and talked with Henri's mom for a few minutes. Then she returned to her lakeside home.

"Did you have a good time?" her mother asked. "What did you do?"

"We had a fabulous spaghetti supper with chocolate cake for dessert. Saturday morning we rowed over to a really pretty cove and had a picnic under a big oak tree. It was wonderful. Can we go back out there next weekend? Gramma said to ask you about it. She said I could bring Erika along and that Joey and a friend could come, too. Please, Mom, can we?"

"Sure, you can ask Erika and I'll talk with Joey. Maybe Joey would like to ask Ben from next door to come along. That'll give him someone to play with."

"That's a great idea. Thanks, Mom!"

11

AFTER RETURNING FROM GRAM'S HOUSE, MRS. HOLLYWELL dropped J.J. off at his house. He had some things to do so the boys made plans to get together later.

J.J.'s mom was coming into the kitchen at the same time he entered from the dining room.

"Hi, Mom," he said as he got a drink of water.

"Hi, J.J. How did things go with Grams?"

"Very well. Everything is okay. I think I'll rest a little before supper."

"Okay. It will be ready in about forty-five minutes."

She started supper while J.J. climbed the stairs to his second-floor bedroom. Jerry's door was open so he spoke to him as he walked by.

"Hi, Jer. Are you in there? Whatcha doin'?"

"Hi, J.J. I'm just playing a video game. Want to come in and play, too?"

"I can't right now. I'm really tired from the walk back to the old forty at Gram's place. We'll have to take you and Joey along next time. I think I'll rest a little before supper. Wake me when Mom calls, will you?"

"Sure thing. That would be great. Could we go to the old swimming hole? That would be a lot of fun!" exclaimed Jerry.

As he lay down, J.J. started thinking about the stone. He wondered what kind of power it had and would he be able to use it. He also wondered if it was just a joke being played on him by a long dead great-grandfather. He'd know soon enough.

He had to figure out how to boil the stone without anyone knowing. The kitchen was open and someone might see him if he did it while anyone was home. Maybe an opportunity would present itself and he would find himself the only one in the house.

J.J. fell asleep. He dreamed of having superpowers. He would fly around the world saving people and catching crooks. It was very exciting. Then he accidentally flew into a wall and crashed to the ground with a loud thud!

"What was that crash?" Jerry asked from the doorway. And what are you doing on the floor?"

"Ah, I was looking for something and I slipped," he stuttered. "I'm okay." He looked at his clock. "Is supper ready?"

"I'll go check," Jerry volunteered.

He felt really silly having fallen out of bed onto the hardwood floor. His head hurt a little. He must have bumped it when he landed. What a dummy! That must have been some dream, although he could not remember any of it.

"Supper's nearly ready," called Jerry from the bottom of the stairs. "Come down in five minutes."

"Okay," J.J. called from his doorway. He brushed his hair somewhat back into place and went down the stairs.

Mom was just taking up the hamburger patties from the frying pan. She stacked four of them onto a plate. Then she placed them on the table next to the buns and potato chips. There were sweet pickles and creamed corn there, too.

"How about chocolate milk to drink, guys?" she asked.

"Chocolate for me," Jerry said as he sat down at the table.

"I'll have regular milk," J.J. offered.

They all sat down to eat. When they had finished mom brought out a fresh apple pie from the oven.

"I'll get the ice cream," Jerry said as he got up.

They had hot apple pie with ice cream melting over it. "Mom, you sure are a good cook," a stuffed J.J. complimented.

"I'll second that. Thanks, Mom," chimed in Jerry.

"You're both welcome. It's nice to feel appreciated," Mom replied.

"Mom, I'm going up to my room to get the things I

need to take to Matt's house," Jerry said as he went up the stairs.

"Okay, but don't be too long," Mom replied.

"Mom, Can I show you something we found at Gram's house?" J.J. asked.

"Sure," she replied.

J.J. pulled the stone bracelet out of his pocket and showed it to his mother. "I found this in the basement in an old trunk with some of Great-grandpa and Great-grandma Jamison's books and Bibles. I liked it. I know I should have asked Grams if I could keep it, but I bet she won't care." He felt a little ashamed.

"You're right. You should have asked her first. Maybe you could apologize to her and then ask about the bracelet. Here, let me see it."

J.J. handed it to her.

After looking it over Mom commented, "I've never seen this before. Where did you say you found it?"

"It was in an old trunk with straps around it. There were old books and a couple of Bibles there, too."

"It just looks like an old bracelet with a dark blue stone. I don't think the stone is anything special or valuable. It looks old and pitted or cracked. I'll bet Grams won't care if you want to wear it."

"Good. Let's go back to see her next weekend."

"Okay. I'll call her and tell her we're coming. J.J., would it be okay if I left you alone for a while? Jerry has asked me to take him over to Matt's house from seven to eight thirty. I think I'll do some shopping and pick him up on the way home."

"Sure, Mom. That'll be all right with me. I think I'll just watch some TV this evening." He could not believe his good fortune. He would get to test the stone this very evening.

At six forty-five Mom and Jerry pulled out of the driveway, leaving J.J. alone in the house. He waited ten minutes to be sure they didn't come back for something. Jerry had a habit of forgetting things when he went places.

When he was sure he was alone, he pulled the bracelet from his pocket. He examined it carefully. Nothing about it had changed.

"Now let's see," he said out loud. "The directions said to push the stone out of the bracelet first. Then I should put it in a pan of water to boil. Then I carefully take it out. As soon as it is cool enough to touch, I should put it back into the bracelet. Then I press my right thumb onto the stone. It's supposed to burn a little bit but not hurt me."

J.J. got out the letter and checked to see if he had remembered correctly. He found he had, so to the kitchen he went.

He got out a pan, filled it half full of water, and set the burner dial to five. His mom had good cookware that could not be heated above five. "This will take too long," he said out loud again. He looked through the lower cabinet and found a seldom used old pan. "I can use this on high heat. It'll only take a couple of minutes to bring it to a boil. Am I really talking out loud to myself?"

So he emptied the first pan and placed it in the dish drainer. He filled the second pan and turned the burner up to nine. Then he waited.

12

AS THE WATER GOT HOTTER A STRANGE THING HAPPENED. The stone got larger and began to glow. The stone was three times its original size and was giving off a bluish light by the time the water started to boil.

J.J. turned the stove off and used two hot pads to remove the stone from the pan. He laid it on a cooling rack and waited some more.

As the stone cooled something like a small screen appeared in the center of the stone. It was about one and one-half inches square. Suddenly a voice called out from the screen.

"Congratulations, Chosen One. You are selected for a most valiant quest. First you must train using the power of this stone from Saros. If you prove worthy, then more information and direction will be given to you."

J.J. did not know what to say.

"Pick me up in your left hand." J.J. trembled a little

as he touched the stone. It should have cooled off by now but it felt hot. The voice continued as he picked up the stone. "You are about to activate the power of the stone. It will have a very powerful force once you have imprinted it. See the small area under the screen? That's where you should press your right thumb."

J.J. did as he was told. He let out a gasp. "Ouch! That's hot!" But he kept his thumb firmly pressed onto the stone. He didn't think he could have removed his thumb if he had tried to. The stone cooled off rapidly after a few moments.

"After the stone has returned to its normal size, place it back into the strap," the voice ordered. "Then place the strap around your left wrist. Do not ever remove the bracelet again!"

J.J. was getting a little worried. "I have been following directions from a talking stone without thinking. And now I am being told to strap this thing to my wrist and to leave it there forever!"

The voice was talking again. "When you use the stone's power, you will be the only one who knows what is happening. You use the power by once again placing your right thumb onto the stone. It will glow and get warm. You will notice something like a blink and there will be a slight flash. This will turn time back one hour. When this happens everything will be as it was one hour earlier. Nothing will change unless you do something to make it change. Anything you do differently will cause everything else to change in relation to what you do. All that happens during the re-lived time will be permanent. You cannot go back and change it again."

J.J. had lots of questions but was afraid to speak.

"That's all you need to know for now. Do not tell anyone about this new ability you have. They will not understand it and you cannot prove it to them because you are the only one who knows when the past hour is being relived."

With that the stone began to lose its glow and shrink in size. In just a few seconds it was back to its original size.

He remembered what to do next and decided to do it. He placed the stone back into the bracelet. And then he strapped the bracelet onto his wrist.

And then it was over. It looked just like any other bracelet with a stone set into it.

"Now that was interesting," he again spoke out loud. "No one is going to believe this. Oh, I can't tell anyone. I can't even tell Mike. I guess I'll just have to say the stone didn't work but that I've decided to wear it because it's been in the family for so long."

As soon as he had washed the old pan and put it away, Mom and Jerry came in. "What have you been doing?" Jerry asked right away.

"I just came down to get a drink," J.J. said weakly. He went to the cupboard and got a glass. Then he got ice and cold water from the front of the refrigerator.

"Why is one of my good pans in the drainer?" Mom inquired. "Were you cooking something?"

Thinking quickly he answered, "I was going to boil some eggs but it takes too long in your cookware. So I didn't. I guess I'm not hungry after all."

"I'm going to play some video games in my room and then I'm going to bed," Jerry announced.

"I think I will look over my geography material for a while before turning in. Good night, Mom." And he followed Jerry upstairs.

"Good night, boys," Mom added as they disappeared around the corner upstairs.

13

MOM LET THE BOYS SLEEP IN THE NEXT MORNING INSTEAD of getting them up for church. They went every Sunday and yesterday J.J. had seemed especially tired. So she left them a note and went to church by herself.

The boys woke up nearly at the same time around nine thirty. They were surprised to see each other coming out of their bedrooms.

"Hi, J.J.," yawned a sleepy Jerry.

"Hi, Jer. Did you hear Mom call us for church?"

"Nope. Let's go downstairs and see what she's doing."

They found Mom's note. So that's why they had slept so long. It felt good to sleep in once in a while. "Let's have oatmeal for breakfast," suggested Jerry.

"Okay. You set the table and I'll make the oatmeal. We will only need bowls and spoons. Maybe you could get some glasses and pour us some orange juice."

"Sure thing. I can do that."

The boys ate a leisurely breakfast and went back to their rooms. The morning flew by as they kept busy with various things they were interested in.

Mom got home around twelve fifteen and started lunch. She called upstairs at twelve forty-five and both boys came down to eat.

The telephone rang just as they were finishing lunch. It was Mike calling for J.J.

"Hi, J.J. Can you come over?"

"Sure. We've just finished lunch so I can come right away."

"Okay. Meet me in the cherry tree."

"Got it."

He had to do some more thinking about what to tell Mike about the bracelet. His previous idea had been to tell him it was all a joke from his great-grandfather. He decided to stick with that story as nothing better came to his mind.

He started out for Mike's house. He slowly walked through the backyard shortcut he favored. It was three times as far if he followed the sidewalk around the block to Mike's house. Mike was his cousin as well as his best friend. Even though they lived in town, the houses here had incredibly large backyards.

There are a lot of trees in these yards. There are two tall cherry trees in Mike's backyard. J.J. and Mike like to climb them and actually somewhat jump from one branch to another. Mike is a better climber than J.J.

"Hi, J.J.," came the call from somewhere among the branches of one of the cherry trees.

"Which tree are you in?"

"Just follow my voice and climb up. You'll find me."

J.J. figured out which tree to climb and started up. He was very careful where he placed his feet. There were a lot of branches so they could stand on one and hold onto a higher branch. It was quite safe that way as long as a foot or hand didn't slip.

There was one set of branches where Mike could reach out, lean forward, and just grab a higher branch with both hands as he fell forward. He had to not miss the branch he was reaching for or he would fall. The ground was ten or eleven feet below. After grabbing the branch when leaning out he could keep his momentum going and swing over and land his feet on the branch a little lower. The branch where his feet landed was too far away to just step over to it.

"Hey, watch this," Mike called out proudly as he leaned forward, reached for and grabbed the branch with both hands. As he swung his feet over, the branch he was holding broke off with a loud crack!

"*Yeow!*" Mike yelled as he fell out of the tree. His feet slid off the branch and he fell straight down. His head bounced off a branch as his back hit another one. Finally he landed on the ground with a thud and didn't move.

"Mike!" screamed J.J. "Can you hear me? Are you

all right?" J.J. tried to climb down the tree quickly, but he had to do so safely. Mike was still not moving when he finally got to the ground.

"Talk to me, Mike," he pleaded with fear in his voice. "Can you move? Oh God! This can't be happening!"

Mike didn't move as J.J. thought about what to do. He didn't know if he should do CPR or run to the house for help. He put his face next to Mike's chest. Mike wasn't breathing. He could not feel or hear Mike's heart beating. Mike was dead!

Tears flooded J.J.'s eyes. His cousin and best friend was dead. And there was nothing he could do about it. As he rubbed the tears from his eyes, something brushed against the side of his face. It was rough and scratchy. And then he remembered . . . the bracelet!

14

ERIKA WAS STUDYING HER MATH WHEN SHE GOT THE URGE TO call Henri. It was nearly eight o'clock Sunday evening and there was school the next day.

"Hello," answered Henri.

"Hi, Henri. It's Erika. How was your surprise from your mom?"

"Oh, it was very nice. Gramma Tessie wanted me to come out for supper and spend the night on Friday. Then on Saturday we took a boat ride to a new beach and picnic area she recently had built. She asked me to invite you to go out for a swim next weekend. Mom, Joey, and his friend Ben, are invited too. Want to go?"

"Sure. That sounds like fun. I'll ask my mom and dad about it. I've been doing some math review. Dr. M sure makes it sound easy in class. I wanted to go over it yesterday and today to be sure I understand it."

"I've been reading some for my last book report of the year. I only have twenty pages left to finish my book. That report form Dr. M uses sure makes reporting easy. All you have to do is read the book and tell him the few things he wants to know about it. I wish all teachers could explain things so I can understand like he does."

"Yes, this has been a good year. I'll miss his class when we move to middle school next year. I sure wish he could move up with us."

"Next year will be different, that's for sure. We'll have six teachers to work for instead of just one who really cares about us," Henri remarked with a long sigh.

"It will all work out okay," added Erika. "See you at school tomorrow."

Henri discovered after she hung up that it had gotten dark. She hurried up to her room. There was a necklace in her top drawer she could hardly wait to get her hands on.

She felt herself trembling as she pulled the necklace from between her shirts where she had hidden it. "It's time to see what this is all about," she said to no one in particular. "I want to believe Gramma Tessie, but what she said was a little far out. And yet she didn't really give me much information."

Carefully she locked her bedroom door. Then she turned off the lights. It was not totally dark so she pulled the blinds down on her window. Now it was very dark.

She slowly felt her way back to her bed. She sat

down in the middle of it and felt the necklace in her hands. Nothing about it seemed special. It was just a small heart-shaped dark blue stone on a leatherlike strap. However, she tried hard to believe.

Are you going to do it or not? she thought to herself. Put it in between both hands and close them together tightly were the directions. So she did it.

At first she thought nothing happened. Then her hands began to glow. This frightened her but somehow she remained calm. The glow stopped at her wrists. The stone was glowing also and it was beginning to feel cool in her hands. Slowly she opened her hands as a picture, or more precisely words appeared in the air in front of her. She read them in a whisper.

"You have been selected as the bearer of the necklace of Saros. Keep it with you always. It has the power to stop time. You stop time by pressing your two thumbs together on the front and back of the stone. The stoppage of time will be for one hour. Nothing will happen during that time. You will be the only one who can move then. Use that time wisely. Anyone you touch during that time will come alive. Use this feature with discretion so no one else will learn of your power.

"You may start time sooner than the one hour by placing your thumbs against the front and back of the stone again. Otherwise time will resume after one hour.

"There is more to this necklace than you now know. More will be revealed to you as you grow in maturity and

use the power of the stone for good. You will be told more when you are ready."

And with that the words disappeared and the glow faded away. Her hands still felt a little cold but otherwise Henri felt normal. The surprise came when she noticed that nearly an hour had passed since she had taken the necklace out of her drawer. It felt like only a few minutes.

She decided the only thing she could do was put the necklace on over her head and around her neck. It disappeared behind her sweatshirt. It felt like it wasn't even there. She touched it through her shirt with her hand. Yes, it was still there.

She unlocked her door and went downstairs. It was nearly nine o'clock. Where did the time go?

Funny, she thought. *Time is such an important thing and we all let it pass by us.*

"Hi, honey," said her mom startling Henri. "Are you okay? You look a little peaked."

"I'm fine. Just a little tired and thirsty."

"Get yourself a drink and then off to bed with you. There are only a few more weeks of school before summer break. You don't want to get sick."

"Okay," she replied. She got her drink and decided to take it upstairs with her. "Good night, Mom. See you in the morning."

"Good night," Mom answered back.

15

THE BRACELET WAS RIGHT THERE ON J.J.'S WRIST. HE WAS still in shock!

What do I do? he wondered. He forced himself to remember the instructions for using the stone. Then he became very calm.

"Place my right thumb firmly into the indentation on the stone," he said out loud, "and hope."

Nothing. And then his thumb got warm and there was a sort of flash before his eyes. It was like a blink.

What's this? he thought to himself. J.J. was sitting at the table with his mom.

"Mom, can I show you something I found at Gram's house?" J.J. asked.

"Sure," she replied.

J.J. pulled the stone bracelet out of his pocket and handed it to his mother. "I found this in the basement in an old trunk with some of Great-grandpa and Great-grandma Jamison's books and Bibles. I liked it. I know I should have asked Grams if I could keep it, but I bet she won't care." He felt a little ashamed.

"You're right. You should have asked her first. Maybe you could apologize to her and then ask about the bracelet. Here, let me see it."

After looking it over, Mom commented further, "I've never seen this before. Where did you say you found it?"

"It was in an old trunk with straps around it. There were old books and a couple of Bibles there, too," J.J. replied.

"It just looks like an old bracelet with a dark blue stone. I don't think the stone is anything special or valuable. It looks old and pitted or cracked. I'll bet Grams won't care if you want to wear it."

"Good. Let's go back and see her next weekend."

"Okay. I'll call her and tell her we're coming."

The phone rang just as they were finishing lunch. It was Mike calling for J.J. "Hi, J.J. Can you come over?"

"Sure, we've just finished lunch and I can come right away."

"Okay. Meet me in the cherry tree."

"Got it."

It was then that he realized what was happening. He knew he was reliving what had happened an hour ago. Now he knew the stone really did stop time and send it back an hour. But the real test would be if he could save Mike.

He hurried through the backyards on the shortcut

he favored. Even though this was a shortcut, it seemed to take forever to get to Mike's house. The two cherry trees came into view as he came around the neighbor's backyard garage. When he got closer he heard Mike's voice again calling to him.

"Hi, J.J.," came the call from somewhere among the branches of one of the trees.

Now we see if I can change things, he thought. "Are you in the first tree?" he asked.

"Yeah. How did you know? Can you see me?"

This was a different response from Mike. That means at least our conversation has been changed, he thought again.

"No! But please do not climb or move until I get up there with you." Quickly but carefully he climbed up to where Mike was. However this time he climbed up opposite where he had climbed before. This put him right where Mike was ready to jump. He was careful not to grab the branch that had broken before.

"Hey! Get out of the way!" shouted his perturbed friend. "You're right where I want to do my famous jump."

"This is important, Mike. What would happen if you missed the branch when you jump?"

"I would probably fall and really get hurt. But I've never missed."

"You could even be killed," J.J. corrected. "It's over ten feet to the ground. And look at all the branches in the way between here and the ground that you would hit while falling."

"Come on, let me jump!" Mike was quite insistent.

"What if the branch breaks? You've probably weakened it by jumping and grabbing it so many times. And besides, don't make fun of this. I had a dream last night about you falling out of this cherry tree."

"You don't believe in that sort of thing, do you?"

"Not usually, but you are my best friend and I sure wouldn't want anything to happen to you. I'd feel terrible if something bad I dreamed about happened to you and I didn't try to stop it."

"Okay. I can see I'm not going to win this argument. Why don't you carefully reach up and pull on my branch. Then you will see there was nothing to worry about?"

"Sure." Slowly he reached up with one hand while holding on tight with the other. He knew what was going to happen and did not want to lose his balance when the branch broke off. "Here goes." He pulled down on the branch right where Mike usually grabbed it. Then he let some of his weight pull it down while maintaining his balance.

Crack!!! Came the sound he expected.

"What?" exclaimed Mike. "Oh my God! The branch broke! I could have been killed! How did you know that? Did that bracelet tell you?"

"No, the bracelet did not tell me. I've been worried about your jumping around in this old tree for a long time. And that crazy dream last night. I'm surprised I just remembered it as I climbed into the tree. I usually don't remember my dreams. Maybe seeing you up here triggered the memory. Anyway, let's carefully climb down and stay out of these trees."

"I'm still shaking from seeing that branch break off. It'll take me a bit to climb down."

"At least you're able to climb down. Let's not tell anyone about this, okay?"

"Okay with me. I would like to forget it altogether."

The two boys decided to get a couple of sodas and sit on the front porch. "Don't worry, no one's home," said Mike. J.J. knew what was coming next. "I see you're wearing that bracelet with the old stone in it. Does it tell you the future?"

"No one can tell the future. It is constantly changing. You know we both decided the bracelet was just a joke from my great-grandfather. I bet he's somewhere in heaven laughing his head off right now."

"I don't know if I believe you. That was a pretty impressive demonstration with that broken branch."

I should have handled this differently, J.J. thought. *Mike is already suspicious. I should have somehow pulled on the branch without telling Mike why. But then Mike could have jumped while I was climbing up and been permanently killed this time. I will have to learn more discretion when using the stone in the future.*

"Last night I tried boiling the stone. Nothing happened. I even tried it twice in case I did something wrong. It just got very hot. I picked it up, held it, turned it all around. And still nothing happened." He hated to lie to Mike, but the instructions from the stone had been very precise. He was to tell no one about the power of the stone.

"I guess I believe you. You don't have any reason to lie to me. Best friends don't lie to one another."

Not unless one of their lives depends on it, thought J.J.

They sat on the porch, drank their sodas, and talked about lots of other things. They talked about the trip back out to Gram's house to swim next weekend.

"Mom was a little upset with me for taking the bracelet. She said I would have to apologize to Grams and tell her about how and where we found it. Then I could ask if I could keep it. I don't think she will care, especially if I apologize."

"She probably won't even remember the bracelet. Maybe your great-grandfather never showed it to her."

"We'll find out on Saturday. Want to throw the football around a little?"

"Sure. We need to get some kind of exercise, since tree climbing has been eliminated."

"Very funny."

The boys tossed the football around for a few minutes. Then Harold, a college junior who lived next door, came out. He played quarterback while Mike and J.J. went one-on-one trying to catch passes. They had a great time for over an hour. When they got tired they sat back on the porch and talked some more.

Harold had to go in to get ready for work. He worked at the local hardware store five days a week. College was already out for the summer and they held this job for him every year. He started working there during his junior year in high school. He was very knowledgeable about tools, plumbing, and things electrical.

Mike's mom and his brother Daryl got home right after they had returned to the porch. "Is that all you guys do," joked Daryl, "just sit around on the porch and drink pop?"

"Hey, we climbed the cherry tree and played an hour of football with Harold. Get off our case!" Mike said, and laughed.

"Just kidding around," responded Daryl, laughing himself.

J.J. decided it was time for him to go home. Walking around the long way following the sidewalk sounded good to him. It would give him some time to think. And he surely needed that right now.

16

THE NEXT DAY DR. M ANNOUNCED THE GEOGRAPHY QUIZ again. This was the week for it. It would be tomorrow, Tuesday, right after lunch. He often gave quizzes then. He said it gave the kids time to unwind and also some extra time to study. On the contrary he only gave tests in the middle of the morning. He would always give students time to review and study right before a test. He said they were fresher and did better work in the morning.

"Everyone try to pick someone you have not worked with for a long time. We are going to study together today for about forty-five minutes." This would be when Dr. M answered questions about the quiz as well as asked questions the students answered.

Reading followed when geography time was finished. The class was reading a novel together. Each student had a chance to read aloud while everyone else followed along in their books. They were reading a story about the future where suddenly all the adults had died. In the time of two weeks everyone over the age of twelve was gone. Some sort of space virus apparently was to blame. This was the story of a twelve-year-old girl who used her ingenuity and bravery to save herself, her little sister, and eventually an entire town of kids. She even overcame an eleven-year-old bully-type boy who had formed a gang and stole from everyone else. The class paid attention to this story because they really liked the idea of kids running things. Plus there would be a test on the book when they finished it.

The next day arrived with the kids in Dr. M's class a little nervous. They had studied and were all well prepared. But they still dreaded quizzes and tests.

There was the usual prepping and studying at lunchtime. Then Dr. M said, "Ten more minutes to study before the quiz. Ask me anything about it."

"Give us the answers," shouted show-off Bill.

"That's not a question," responded Dr. M.

"Will you give us the answers?" corrected Jim.

"No, not just the answers by themselves. But if you ask a question, I'll help arrive at the correct answer. Even if it's an actual quiz question. So ask away."

Several of the smarter girls in class had been looking up items they thought would be good quiz questions. They based these on the areas the class had been studying together with Dr. M.

Up went Sarah's hand. "I have a question."

"Go ahead," Dr. M encouraged.

"What is the name of the large sea north of Africa and southeast of France, Spain, and Italy?"

"Anyone in the class know this one?" asked Dr. M. Bob's hand went up. "Go ahead, Bob."

"The Mediterranean Sea."

"Correct."

Next up was Barbara's hand. Dr. M nodded to her, so she asked her question. "Egypt and the Sudan are on the northeast corner of Africa. Across a long sea is Saudi Arabia. Name this long, large sea."

J.J.'s hand went up and Dr. M indicated he should answer. "The Red Sea."

"That's correct again. See, this is easy," Dr. M said with a smile. "Who's next?"

Billy had the next question. "While we are in the area, what is the large island off the southeastern coast of Africa?"

"I know that one. Disneyland!" shouted out Jack. He was a bit of a clown.

"Jack. You must stand up for the next two questions for wasting our time with that answer."

"Yes, sir," he replied as he stood up.

"I know," volunteered Betty. "I think it's Madagascar. Isn't there a movie by that name?"

"You are right, twice. Now here's one from me," Dr. M continued. "Name the longest river in the U.S. and where does it flow to?"

Cameron had this answer, "That's an easy one.

That would be the Mississippi River and it flows into the Gulf of Mexico," he said proudly.

"Good job. Sam, do you have a question?"

"Can anyone name the five Great Lakes and tell which state they nearly surround?"

"That's an easy one. It's Michigan," said Gail. "The lakes can be remembered by using the acronym HOMES: Huron, Ontario, Michigan, Erie, and the biggest and deepest is Superior."

"Which state is Yellowstone National Park in?" someone asked.

"Wyoming," someone else answered.

"What city is the Golden Gate Bridge in?"

"San Francisco," came the answer.

The questions were coming quite fast now as well as the answers. As long as things were under control, Dr. M let the kids call out questions and answers.

"Nearly all of South America speaks Spanish. What is the one country there where another language is the official language. And name that language," asked Tory.

"Brazil. And the language is Portuguese."

"Technically the second half of that question is not a place. But you could have asked where the people came from who settled in that country," corrected Dr. M.

"Portugal," Pam called out.

"Two more questions and then we take the quiz,"

"What is the ocean that surrounds the North Pole?"

"The Arctic Ocean."

And the last question was asked by Margaret. "What is the second largest ocean in the world?"

"The Atlantic Ocean," the whole class answered together.

"Everyone put away your study sheets and take out just a pencil. I'll pass the quiz out, you fill in the answers, and put your paper in the basket on my desk when you finish. What's the first thing you do when you get your paper, class?"

"Pray?" asked Jean. She was the smartest girl in the class.

"Put your name on it and date it," the rest of the class answered in unison.

The quiz went smoothly. Most students had the twenty-five questions answered in less than ten minutes. Hopefully their speed indicated that they knew the material and were not just hurrying to get finished.

Dr. M gave the class five minutes of free time when everyone was finished and all papers were handed in. The students could walk around the room and talk for these five minutes to sort of unwind from the quiz-taking trauma.

SSR time came along again and another school day ended. There weren't many days of school left before summer vacation.

17

RIGHT AT THREE O'CLOCK DR. M GOT A CALL OVER THE IN-tercom asking him to report to the front office. As soon as the last student had left his room, he walked over to the office. It was right near his room.

The secretary greeted him, "Hi, Dr. Emory. Go right in. The principal is expecting you."

As Dr. Emory entered the office, he was surprised to see Major Stromberg sitting across the desk from Principal Green. Both men got up as he approached them. He shook hands with Major Stromberg and all three sat down.

"There seems to be a small problem," Dr. Green started out. "It seems the federal government has an urgent need for your services, Dr. Emory. This is high-ly unusual. They have already called you away twice this year. The school board approved adding the sec-ond leave without much prodding on my part. That was one more time than the government agreed to take you away from your classroom. Now with only a few days remaining in the school year, they want you again. What's going on?"

"Let me try to explain that," Major Stromberg interrupted. "You understand this conversation we are about to have does not go beyond this room, gentlemen?" The other two men both nodded. "Okay. It's been reported to us that there have been numerous disturbances in the atmosphere above northeastern Russia. Strange shafts of light have been sighted. The locals are scared and the Russian government has asked us to help. Some of the locals have been found dead for no apparent reason with no cause of death determined. Their hearts just stopped beating! A few people have been reported missing.

"This has the backing of the President of the United States as well as the President of Russia. It is being classified as Top Priority and possibly our own national defense could be threatened."

"So what do I tell the students and parents?" Dr. Green wanted to know.

"I do not see that as a problem," Dr. Emory jumped in. "Most of the teachers are wrapping things up for the year. We only have one more test before we start reviewing as part of our prep for middle school. I'm sure my regular substitute can handle things. And I should be back within a week to ten days. I can wrap up the year then without any trouble," he continued. "Why don't we put this down as unpaid leave for an out-of-town emergency? That way no one should question it."

"We want you to leave tonight. Can your substitute be ready by tomorrow?" Major Stromberg asked.

"He is always ready. Plus I have lesson plans on the computer as well as printed out for the rest of the year. There should be no interruption in the students' learning," Dr. Emory concluded.

Major Stromberg got up, shook hands with the principal, and headed for the door. "We'll pick you up at the usual place at the usual time, Dr. Emory." And he walked out the door. The meeting was over.

Still in the office and in somewhat a state of shock, the principal was sweating profusely. "This job is going to be the death of me yet, David. The kids, teachers, and parents I can handle. It's the government I don't understand. Are you the only person in the entire country who can handle this situation? Don't get me wrong, David, but why are you so special?"

"Don't you get me wrong, my friend, but that's classified," David said with a disarming smile. "I need to get home and pack a few things. I only have a few hours to prepare."

The first thing Dr. M did when he got to his car was drive to the parking lot of the high school just a couple of miles away. He parked at the far end away from all the other cars. Then he got out of his car and walked twenty yards away from it. He took out his cell phone and punched in a number he had memorized.

A female voice answered on a special cell phone she kept very well hidden. "Yes?" was all she said.

"We have to meet tonight at seven. The day is not yet over." And he hung up.

He punched in another memorized number and another special phone was answered by a different female voice. He repeated the same message and hung up.

Dr. M got back into his car and drove home. It was only three fifteen but he had a lot to do before the seven o'clock meeting. Then he had to get ready to get to the pickup point by ten o'clock. It would only take him ten minutes to get to the seven o'clock meeting place. It would take him two hours to get from there to the ten o'clock pickup point. But he had to go home and pack first. This was going to be a long journey!

18

HENRI AND ERIKA MET AT THE FRONT OF THE SCHOOL IN their usual place. "Let's stop by the corner convenience store and get an energy drink. I feel kind of tired and don't feel like sitting at Deano's," said Henri.

"That's fine with me," replied Erika. The girls waved to some other students as they turned the corner and headed through the neighborhood toward Joe's Market. The convenience store was only five blocks away right on their way home. "Did you ask your mom about the swim party?"

"Yes. Unfortunately Gramma Tessie had something come up for this weekend. She said she would put us on the calendar for a week from tomorrow."

"That's probably better. I still have to finish my final book report. I wish I hadn't waited so long to read that book."

"Good. That will give you time to read. Would you like to come over to my place tomorrow? We could read together on the back porch."

"That would be great. That way I won't be able to put it off again," she sighed.

"Oh, Mom said Gramma Tessie suggested that maybe we would like to ride our bikes out to her place on Friday. She has room in her Tahoe for them when she brings us back Saturday afternoon. Then we would wake up at the lake on Saturday morning."

"Oh, I would really like to do that," exclaimed Erika with a big smile. "I'm sure Mom and Dad will approve."

The girls walked another couple of blocks enjoying the 72-degree temperature. Some of the larger trees completely covered the narrow street, making it feel like they were in a forest. There were lilies and marigolds blooming with vivid colors in several well-manicured lawns. This was a very nice neighborhood.

The girls saw the business district coming up as they finished their five-block walk. The convenience store was on the corner where the houses ended and the businesses began.

There was a drive-through gas station across the street from Joe's Market where they were headed. A quilting shop was across the corner followed by several other businesses on both sides of the street.

"Looks like we will have the place to ourselves," commented Erika as they walked into the empty parking lot. "No cars parked out front. Joe's probably snoozing in his big chair again."

Joe was the owner and usually worked the day shift. He was a pleasant man of about sixty years old. He was a little overweight but was quite agile. He often fell asleep afternoons while sitting behind the counter in his special chair. Everybody loved Joe and he trusted everybody.

He hired a couple of older boys to work along with him on weekends. That was when he got caught up on his ordering and his paperwork. He had a retired postal worker who came in for the night shift. The store closed at midnight and reopened again at six a.m. Bill, an eighteen-year-old just out of high school should be coming to work around 5:00 tonight.

The girls entered the market and saw Joe walking toward his chair. "Hi, Joe," they called out in greeting.

"Hi, Henri. Hi, Erika. School's out already?" he asked. He often lost track of time.

The girls turned up the first aisle and walked toward the back of the store. That was where the cases were with cold drinks in them. While they were deciding what to get to drink, they heard a loud voice shouting, "Okay, old man. Empty the cash drawer! And be quick about it!"

"Sure, sure," Joe said with a quiver in his voice as he was getting up from his chair. His feet slipped off the rung of his chair and he crashed to the floor.

The robber must have thought Joe was reaching for

a gun so he fired at him. At least that's what the girls thought.

Bang! Bang! Bang! The noise was deafening in the small store. Erika and Henri had moved behind a rack of chips and things and were huddled together on the floor. "What should we do?" whispered Erika. "I think he shot Joe. He might shoot us if he sees us. I don't want to die." Tears started down her cheeks.

"We are not going to die, Erika," comforted Henri. A strange calmness came over Henri as she thought about what to do. Then she carefully reached inside her blouse and pulled out the necklace. Erika had her face in her hands wiping away the tears and didn't see what Henri was doing.

Next she quickly pressed her two thumbs against the front and back of the stone. There was a sort of flash before her eyes and then something like a blink and that was all.

"Erika," she whispered, "can you hear me?" Erika did not answer. In fact Erika did not even move.

Henri was shocked! *Wow!* she thought. *I think it worked. But that's impossible. Or is it? Only one way to be more sure, I'll have to go to the front of the store.*

She slowly rose and quietly made her way toward the front of the store. It was eerily quiet. As she peeked around the last stack to get a view of the check out counter, she saw a strange sight. There stood a man who looked to be twenty or so years old. He had some kind of mask over his face, a hat pulled down over his eyes, and a gun in his hand pointed over the counter. The hardest part to believe was that he appeared to be frozen in place.

Warily she approached him. He did not move. His eyes were open and his mouth appeared to be stuck in some angry shout. When she was sure he could do her no harm, she went around the corner to look behind the counter. There was Joe lying on the floor on his side. His eyes were open and there was no blood anywhere. The bullets must have missed him as he fell.

"Now what do I do?" she said out loud to herself. "I must be sure not to touch anyone. If the stone works as I was told, I have one hour to try to prevent this robbery and keep everyone alive." Then an idea came to her.

She went to the fountain where drinks were dispensed and got several napkins. Then she approached the man with the gun. Carefully she wrapped the barrel of the gun with a napkin. Then slowly she wiggled it back and forth staying out of the line of fire. She was also careful not to touch the man's fingers. The gun finally came free and it tipped downward while she held it with the barrel facing up. "I hope I don't shoot myself!" She did not want to touch the grip because the man's fingerprints would be there.

"I either have to get this to the police station or put it behind the counter for Joe to see." She chose the first option. She did not want to leave the gun in the store. The police station was just a block away.

She ran all the way there holding the gun out in front of her. She used her shoulder on the door and burst into the police station. She saw several officers there. Some were standing and one was seated at a desk with a telephone to his ear. There was another officer seated at what looked like an information desk. They were all frozen, seemingly suspended in time.

She walked over to the desk where the officer was using the telephone. She saw an open pad of paper sitting on his desk and placed the gun next to it. Using two napkins she held the pad of paper still with one hand and picked up the pen from the officer's desk with the other. Then she wrote this note:

HELP!

THERE IS A ROBBERY IN PROGRESS AT JOE'S MARKET ON MAIN STREET. THIS IS THE GUN THE ROBBER WAS USING. PLEASE COME QUICKLY. SHOTS WERE FIRED!

She tried to print the note with a different style of printing than she normally used. She did not want anyone to match it to hers. She placed the note on the officer's desk next to the gun. Hopefully he would see it as soon as time started up again. Now she was ready to go back to the convenience store.

Henri decided to take the pen with her. It could be disposed of into a trashcan somewhere later. It was difficult, but she used one of the napkins to pull the door open so she could leave. Wondering what she should do next she started back toward Joe's.

She knew she had plenty of time, so she went down a side street past a couple of stores. There were trashcans in front of several stores. One was nearly overflowing. She pulled out a brown bag and slipped the pen from the police station inside. Once again she was careful to use a napkin and not get any prints on either the pen or the trashcan. Henri pushed the bag way down into the trashcan and then hurried back to Joe's.

Everything was still the same there. "I wonder if Joe keeps a gun behind the counter?" When she got back to Joe's, she looked. Sure enough, there was a gun right on a shelf in front of where Joe had fallen. If he had tried to grab that gun, the robber might have killed him.

"I guess there's nothing left for me to do." So she returned to Erika. "Now I should try to start time up again," she said. "Hope I did things right."

Henri pulled the necklace out and pressed both thumbs together on both sides of it. Another flash of light and then a blink followed. Erika's hands moved.

Quickly she put the necklace back inside her blouse. "Erika, it's going to be okay," she whispered and put her arms around her.

"Come on, old man!" yelled the would-be robber as he leaned over the counter. "Get up here and put your hands where I can see them. What the? Where's my gun? What happened to my gun?"

Joe had recovered from his fall and reached out and picked up his gun. He got up and aimed it at the confused robber.

"That's enough now. It's over. Put up your hands," Joe ordered.

Instead of raising his hands the man turned and raced for the door. He pulled the door open and ran outside.

Joe did not want to shoot the man in the back. So he held his fire. His camera would get a partial description of him and maybe the police could track him down.

The robber was very surprised when he turned to run. He ran right into a uniformed Millville police officer. The officer wrestled him to the ground and cuffed him. "You're under arrest for attempted robbery," the officer said. And then he read him his rights.

The other four officers who had run from the station called out to anyone inside the convenience store. "Anyone inside the store, come out with your hands up."

"Everything is all right now, officers," shouted Joe from inside. "It's me, Joe Martin. I own this store. There was only one robber. I'm coming out now." Joe had been smart enough to leave his gun behind the counter.

"Is anyone else inside the store?" the sergeant asked.

"Yes, and I imagine those two girls hiding in the back are pretty scared. They are back by the pop cooler. They were back there when the robber came in. He never saw them."

"Thanks," Sergeant Mills said. "We'll check on them." They found Henri and Erika still holding each other cuddled together on the floor. "It's all right now, girls. It's over. The suspect has been arrested. Let's get you two outside into the fresh air. Give us your phone numbers and we will call your parents. Everything will be okay. The robber never saw you."

He and another officer helped the girls up and took them outside. They let them sit down on the curb in the shade. Another officer brought them bottles of water.

"This is the most exciting drink of water I ever got at Joe's," remarked Erika, trying to inject some humor into the situation. She seemingly was recovering quickly from her experience.

"I'll second that," added Henri.

Both Henri's mom and Erika's mom arrived a few minutes later. Luckily no other customers had come into the store. So no one knew the girls had sort of seen the robbery.

"Henri, are you all right?" asked a nervous Mrs. Matthews. "What happened?"

"Sure, Mom. I'm fine. It was nothing. The police arrived to save the day," she replied with relative calm.

Mrs. Sorenson asked her daughter the same questions and got a little different answer. "I was scared stiff!" Erika replied.

How appropriate, thought Henri, remembering what Erika looked like frozen in time.

"Let's get you girls home," Mrs. Sorenson said with final authority.

"We would like to come by in a few minutes and get statements from each girl," Sergeant Mills stated. "We will be right over after we finish up here. Give me your names and addresses, please."

After giving him the information, the mothers took their daughters home. The police came by just a little later and asked the girls several questions. The only information of value was that they had heard what the robber had yelled at Joe and that they had heard three gunshots. Their stories each matched what Joe had told the police.

Mrs. Sorenson called Mrs. Matthews right after the police left. "How about you and Henri come over here in an hour for pizza? We can talk with the girls together."

"That's a great idea, thanks."

Henri's mom then called the neighbor two doors over. "We have an important errand to run. Could you watch Joey for a couple of hours for me, please? I'll spring for the pizza for the boys."

"Sure," the neighbor replied. "Tim will be glad to have Joey to play with. Send him over whenever you are ready to leave."

"Thanks." Mrs. Matthews replied. "Henri, we're going over to Erika's house for pizza in an hour, okay?"

"Sure, Mom. I'd like to talk with her anyway."

19

THERE WAS A LOT OF DISCUSSION HAPPENING AT THE POLICE station after the robbery.

"How did that revolver get on my desk?" Officer Cole was asking. "And that note about the robbery, where did that come from?"

Lieutenant McNeil had come in from his office in the back. He was in charge. He asked, "Did any of you see anyone come in and leave the gun and the note?" No one had seen anything.

"Did you check the cameras?" Officer Jones asked.

"We just did," Lt. McNeil responded. "There is a tiny blip in the film about the time officer Cole found the note on his desk. There was nothing else on the film other than our own police officers. No one approached Officer Cole's desk during that time. And no one entered or left the building during the time of the attempted robbery."

"What's with that little blip?" Officer Cole wanted to know.

"The recorder got everything up to and after the blip. There is less than a one second loss in time on the tape. There is no clear view of your desk, so we do not know how or when the gun and note appeared."

"Did you check Joe's video camera at the store?" asked Officer Nick Cole.

"That's next on my list. Nick, you take Stan and get that video from Joe."

"Yes, sir," he replied. The two officers left immediately to drive to Joe's Market to get that very important video.

Fifteen minutes later the two officers returned with the video from Joe's store camera.

"What does it show?" Lieutenant McNeil asked.

"You're not going to believe it," Officer Cole stated. "You will have to see it for yourself."

They were in the video room two minutes later. The video started with the two girls walking into the store and greeting Joe. About a minute after the girls were out of the picture, the robber comes in. It shows him pulling his gun and yelling at Joe. Then Joe slips and the robber shoots three times. After a slight blip in the picture the video continues. The time stamp shows it only lasts one second.

When the video resumes, the robber's gun is gone and he is yelling, "Come on, old man! Get up here and put your hands where I can see them! What the? Where's my gun? What happened to my gun?"

Next it shows Joe pointing his gun at the robber and the robber is seen running out of the picture.

"Now that's a mystery," said Officer Jones. "Can you explain that? How can his gun just disappear? That looks like the same kind of blip that was on our video."

"Yes, I think you are right," added Lieutenant Mc-Neil. "Not much can happen in one second. That's not enough time for someone to take the gun from Joe's and bring it here. Maybe someone altered the two re-cordings. But who would do that and why?"

"I can't think of any way anyone could do that," commented Nick.

"Me either," said Stan. The two officers looked at each other and shook their heads. They had stopped the robbery but so many questions remained.

"We'll keep investigating and see what happens. I want to know if there are any fingerprints on that gun. It has been sent to ballistics. We'll know some-thing soon. Maybe the person who brought it here left prints behind. We dug the bullets from the wall at Joe's Market. We will check to see if they were fired from that same gun. We will also check for prints on Officer Cole's desk, the note, and the front door. The forensics team is on the way."

A couple of hours later they had finished getting the prints from the gun. There was no match in their database. The would-be robber apparently did not have a police record. The prints on the gun did match the prints taken from the robber when he was booked into the jail. And the bullets from the wall at Joe's were fired from that gun!

After dusting for prints on the desk and the front door, the only prints they found were their own police officers' prints. There were no prints on the note.

Lieutenant McNeil went back to his office. Now he had another mystery to solve. He wondered out loud, "How did the robber's gun fire bullets into the wall at Joe's and then get to the police station and onto Officer Cole's desk without anyone seeing it happen? How did the robber lose his gun while attempting to rob the market? And who wrote the note that thwarted the robbery and helped to catch the thief? Then there were the blips on the videos." He sure had a lot to think about.

Lieutenant McNeil and the other officers did not know it, but this was one mystery they would never solve!

20

THE MATTHEWS AND SORENSON FAMILIES HAD A WONDERFUL pizza supper together. It was just Henri, her mom, Mr. and Mrs. Sorenson, and Erika at the Sorensons' house for the evening.

"Weren't you girls scared?" asked Mrs. Matthews.

"I sure was," replied Erika, still somewhat shaken from the events earlier that afternoon at Joe's place. "I thought we were going to die!"

"I was really scared, too," added Henri.

"But you told me not to be afraid. I remember you said we were not going to die."

"I was just trying to be brave. I was just as scared as you were, Erika. I was just hoping the robber would take the money from the cash register and run away. Then he would never know we were hiding in the back of the store. So I figured we were reasonably safe."

"You girls still were very brave. If you had made any noises the robber might have shot you. I'm proud of you both for being able to hide and keep quiet," complimented Mrs. Matthews.

If only she knew what had really happened during that attempted robbery. Then she would really be proud of her daughter. However that was not to be.

"She's right," Mr. Sorenson added. "You did the right thing by staying quiet and hidden. Do you think you both will be able to sleep tonight?"

"Oh, I think so. At least no one was killed and they caught the robber. Do you know how the police got there so fast?" asked Erika.

"No. They didn't say," replied Mrs. Sorenson. "Maybe Joe had one of those silent burglar alarms that contacts the police department. I'd have one if I owned a convenience store like his."

"I'm sure we will be just fine," Henri concluded. "Maybe Erika and I could eat out on the back porch and talk some more."

"That'd be great," Erika said as she picked up her plate, grabbed a pop, and headed out back. Henri followed her out.

When the girls had left, Mrs. Sorenson asked, "Don't you think we should pay special attention to our girls for a while?"

"Yes, I do," replied Henri's mom. "However they are both quite resilient and they will bounce back from this quickly. And with school getting out in a few days, they'll be able to spend a lot of time together. That should help a lot."

"I think you're right," agreed Erika's mom. "Summer vacation is coming at just the right time."

The adults agreed it was best if they never talked about the robbery with anyone else. The robber did not know the girls were in the store, and because they couldn't identify him, the police did not need them as witnesses.

Out on the porch talk soon turned to more pleasant things. There was the swim party next weekend to plan. And summer vacation would be here soon. With school out the two girls would probably spend a lot of time together. This was going to be a wonderful summer.

The next day Henri and Erika were sitting at a booth at Deano's when J.J. and Mike walked in. "Hey guys. Come join us," called Henri. "Just think. We only have a few more days of school left. Let's try to do some things together over the summer," suggested J.J.

"Great idea," the other three replied.

After the four of them had ordered their sodas and bowls of ice cream, Mike asked, "Did you guys hear about the fight on the corner of the schoolyard by the middle school? A seventh grader from the middle school walked onto our campus and pushed down a fourth grader who was cleaning up litter on the playground. The seventh grader was much bigger and said threatening things to the little guy."

"No, I didn't hear about that," both girls said at the

same time.

"I heard all about it from Joe," J.J. joined in. "He said he was there and told me every little detail. He and Bob, another sixth grader, were out picking up some PE equipment. They saw the little kid get pushed down. So they ran over to try to help.

"Joe said Bob ran right up to the seventh grade boy and told him to get off the property. He also told him to stop bullying other kids! The bully made the mistake of moving toward Bob to try to push him to the ground.

"Bob grabbed his arm, pulled the bully forward, and fell backward to the ground, pulling the bully with him. The bigger kid was pulled off balance and fell forward. As he was falling, Bob put both feet into the bully's stomach. He let go with his hands and pushed with his feet. The bully went flying head over heels. Quickly Bob got up and backed away a little.

"The bully was so mad he jumped up and ran back toward Bob again. This time Bob side stepped out of the way, stuck out his foot, and tripped the older boy. The seventh grade boy got up swearing at the younger kids.

"That was when Dr. M appeared. None of the boys saw him coming. 'What's going on here?' he asked. 'Martin, what are you doing on the elementary school campus? You know you are not supposed to be here!'

"Before he could answer, Terry, the fourth grader

who was pushed to the ground by Martin, spoke up. 'He pushed me down and was threatening to beat me up. Joe and Bob came to my rescue. Bob told Martin to leave and quit bullying other kids. That was when Martin tried to push Bob down.'

"'Yes, I saw that part,' Dr. M stated. 'Nice moves, Bob. Now Martin, what do you have to say for yourself?'

"'I'm sorry, Dr. Emory. I guess I just got carried away. It won't happen again.'

"'Let's hope not. Joe and Bob, you get your work done and get back inside. It is almost dismissal time.'

"'Sure thing, Dr. M,' they replied.

"'Thanks guys,' Terry said to Joe and Bob.

"'You're welcome,' they said together.

"'Martin, you need to come with me. You will have to talk with Dr. Green. I'm sure he will want to talk with your parents about this.'

"And that was the end of it," J.J. concluded.

"How does Dr. M always seem to be in the right spot to help out?" Henri wondered.

"Yes," added Mike. "He seems to know just what to say and diffuses the situation with such ease. I sometimes think he has special powers."

"That would be way cool," said Erika. All four kids just looked at each other for several minutes.

Epilogue

"TESS, SUPPOSE YOU START," DR. M REQUESTED.

"I have met with Henri this past week. She is now in possession of the necklace. She was quite skeptical but she has now become a believer. She activated the stone and has already used its power to save a life. As a matter of fact, she has just saved Joe's life at the convenience store. She has shown a lot of spunk and ingenuity in doing so. She will become a very important asset."

Grams was next to speak. "J.J. also now has his Saros stone. He had his best friend along when he got it, which we had meticulously planned. He has activated its power and has already used it to save his friend's life. He is learning very quickly and also will be a very powerful team member. When Mike had his accident and was killed, I thought he was out of the picture. I had high hopes for him. Then when J.J. found a way to save him, I knew he was meant to join us."

"I must return to Saros tonight. There have been

some significant developments. There is more talk and plans are being made for an invasion. The water shortage is getting more serious. While I am there I will pick up two more stones. One will be for Mike. Have you determined who the fourth member of the team will be?"

"Erika," they both said at the same time.

"Good. Then we are done for now. I will contact you when I return to Earth."

And so ends the beginning of the discoveries and adventures featuring J.J. Jamison and his friends.

. . . .

To see what adventure lies just ahead, read the following excerpt from book 2.

. . . .

THE LAST DAY OF SCHOOL HAD FINALLY ARRIVED AT MILLVILLE Elementary School. Dr. Green had announced last week that the fourth, fifth, and sixth graders would have a picnic in the afternoon on the last day of school. It would last from twelve thirty until two thirty out on the field. He also reminded everyone of the class races that would take place at two o'clock.

The weather cooperated and the temperature was topping out at a perfect 72 degrees. It was a beautiful day to be outside. All the teachers had organized things for their classes to do. Some played softball, some kickball, and some soccer. One class had set up on the basketball court and was having shooting contests. Everyone was having a great time.

At 1:50 Dr. Green used his bullhorn and called everyone over to the field where the races were to be run. Each class had selected their fastest boy and girl for a race two times around the cones set up around the field. The distance would be somewhere around a quarter of a mile, maybe just a little less. The girls would run first. Then the boys would run. Dr. Green had no idea disaster was about to strike!

"He's dead! I think he's dead!" Pat, a fifth-grade student yelled out. He was leaning over the collapsed fourth grade boy on the track. All 350 kids were completely hushed after seeing Sammy fall down on the track during the race and not get up. It happened right in front of the finish line, so most of the kids saw it happen.

Dr. Green quickly rushed over to the fallen student. He lowered his head to check his breathing. Sammy wasn't breathing.

"Here, let me help," ordered Mrs. Matthews who was the school nurse. "I'll start CPR. Dr. Green, you call 9-1-1."

"Okay," he replied still shaken by what had happened. After calling 9-1-1 on his cell phone, he announced, "Teachers! Please take your students back into the building and into your classrooms."

Slowly and very quietly the shocked students walked back into the building. There was only a half hour left in the school year and something awful had to happen.

The paramedics arrived in seven minutes. They worked on Sammy for several minutes. "It looks like his heart just stopped beating," one of the paramedics finally said. There's nothing we can do for him. He's dead."

They loaded him onto a stretcher and took him to the ambulance. Then they drove to the hospital.

Sammy's parents had been called right after the 9-1-1 call. They arrived just as the ambulance was pulling away. It was hard for Mrs. Matthews to tell Sammy's parents that their son was dead.

They burst into tears. "Oh no! Not my baby!" screamed Sammy's mother. Her husband put his arm around his wife and led her away. They would follow the ambulance to the hospital.

Meanwhile the students were somewhat in shock in their classrooms. Most of them had heard the student say he thought Sammy was dead before Dr. Green could get to him. Everyone was sad. Many of the students in Sammy's classroom were crying.

The principal was going to have to print out a notice telling about the tragedy very quickly to send home with the students today.

J.J.'s sixth-grade classroom was a little noisy as Dr. M had allowed the students to talk and get their feelings out. But a calmness came over J.J. He was puzzled at the way he felt, sort of detached and apart from everyone in the room.

His seat was in the back of the room, so no one could really see him well.

An idea came to him. *I hope this works,* he thought to himself. He took his right hand and pressed his thumb onto the stone in his bracelet. There it was again. The stone got warm, a flash, and he sort of blinked. . .just like the first time with Mike.

It had only been a half-hour since the accident. He thought it might have been too long, but it hadn't. . .

Suddenly it was one fifty-nine instead of two fifty-nine. The girls were assembling at the starting line. The race was about to start.

"Go!" shouted Dr. Green through his bullhorn. And the race was on.

This race would only take a few minutes to run. Then the boys' race would follow right away.

What can I do? J.J. thought to himself. He could think of nothing that would save poor Sammy's life.

All the students were shouting and screaming at the runners. The fifth-graders were yelling out Sandy's name as she crossed the finish line first.

"Yeah, Sandy!" her classmates yelled. "You sure showed those sixth-graders. Way to go!"

Things were going to happen fast now. Dr. Green already was calling for the boys to line up at the starting line. And there was Sammy right in the middle of the runners. He had to think fast.

He didn't know if he could stop the race. He could yell out "Snake!" and that would disrupt things. But that would just get him in trouble and the race would still be run with the same disastrous result.

Suddenly an idea came to him. He ran as fast as he could to the building and through the outside halls to the office. Luckily the nurse's office was the first room just inside the main doors. He hurried in and there it was right on the wall . . .

TO BE CONTINUED

Made in the USA
Charleston, SC
15 April 2015